LANIGAN AND THE SILENT MOURNER

Shawnee Lanigan is a half-breed man-hunter. He's commissioned by a grieving grandfather to track down Marsh Kennebec, who murdered the old man's daughter and her husband. However, Lanigan finds himself fighting for his life against outlaws and corrupt lawmen attempting to bar his path. He finds the killer but, outnumbered and outgunned, he's soon standing trial for his life before a jury of desperados. If convicted, he will hang. If found innocent, he faces a duel to the death.

RONALD MARTIN WADE

◆

LANIGAN AND THE SILENT MOURNER

Complete and Unabridged

LINFORD
Leicester

First published in Great Britain in 2009 by
Robert Hale Limited
London

First Linford Edition
published 2010
by arrangement with
Robert Hale Limited
London

British Library CIP Data

Wade, Ronald Martin.
  Lanigan and the silent mourner - -.
  (Linford western library)
  1. Western stories.
  2. Large type books.
  I. Title II. Series
  823.9'2–dc22

  ISBN 978–1–84782–967–2

Prologue

Patrick Lanigan heard his mother's real name only once, and even then, his father wasn't sure he pronounced it correctly. In English it was Blue Star, but his father had always called her 'Kiji' because the Algonquin language was too much for his Irish tongue. Hampton Lanigan told his son that he met the girl who was to become Patrick's mother when she came into his trading post with her Shawnee mother. She was fifteen, old enough to marry. Hampton, who was forty-five years old and had lost his wife of twenty years to consumption, was looking for a companion. The young half-Shawnee girl had the facial features of a white woman while her skin was bronze and her hair and eyes were like jet. He made a quick bargain with her mother.

Kiji never knew her father or even his

name. She knew only that he was a white man and he disappeared after planting the seed that became the beautiful girl Hampton Lanigan took as a wife.

In 1849, when Patrick made his appearance in the back room of his father's trading post, Kiji was assisted in the delivery by an old midwife from the local Shawnee tribe who pronounced the proper traditional words over the newborn. The boy grew up strong, running free in the territory; hunting, fishing, playing and wrestling with the Shawnee boys. His mother sometimes took him to tribal meetings where he watched, fascinated, as the braves danced by the light of the tribal fire and the old shaman did his magic. He attended no school; his father taught him to count and add but hadn't the patience or skill to teach him to read. The boy had a good life because the things he was doing without, he didn't even know existed.

Despite their age difference, his

father heaped affection on Patrick's mother and always treated her gently, unlike the treatment exhibited by the tribal braves toward their mates. Hampton cautioned his son always to treat a woman like a lady until she proved otherwise.

Patrick was content in his own paradise until his tenth year, when it all came to an end.

Hampton Lanigan had taken the wagon and had gone to pick up a load of merchandise for the trading post. He went to meet merchants from Texas who brought their loads of goods into the Oklahoma Territory but not as far as the Lanigan Trading Post, which stood near to what was called Shawnee Town. At dark, Patrick and his mother closed the store, ate their supper and went to bed secure in the knowledge that the man of the house would be returning the next day. Patrick, exhausted as usual from the day's activities and blessed with a clear conscience, fell into a deep sleep.

Patrick was awakened in the night by loud voices, one of which was his mother's. They were coming from the front of the store. He lay there listening until he became alarmed at a man's angry voice and his mother's scream, followed by the sound of things falling on the wooden floor.

He leapt from the bed and he rushed to the door. The lantern from the living-quarters sat on a countertop at the store's front. By its light, Patrick saw a great bear of a man on his knees, his hands gripping his mother's shoulders, pounding her head against the floor. He roared, 'Cut me will ya? I'll show you, you wagon-burning, squaw bitch.'

The scene was unreal, like a nightmare, a nightmare that the boy had to end by making the man stop hurting his mother. He grabbed an axe from the barrel where they were displayed at the end of the aisle and ran at the big man. He raised the axe above his head and screamed, 'Stop hurting my mother!'

The big man turned around too late to avoid Patrick's headlong rush. The boy brought the axe down with a strength made deadly by his rage.

The first customer of the morning peered into the store and saw a ghastly sight. Patrick was sitting with his dead mother's bloody head in his lap, talking to her and trying to get her to open her eyes. Her assailant lay close by, an axe buried in his skull.

Later they learned that the man who had killed Kiji was fleeing the Texas authorities for a murder he had committed in Fort Worth, one of scores of desperate men who would pass through the territory hiding from vigilante groups or the authorities, alert for a chance to steal an easy dollar. The Indian Agent, a friend of Hampton's, examined the assailant's body and found the wounds from Kiji's knife.

Kiji's death was too much for Hampton Lanigan to handle. His spirit broken and his health deteriorating, he found a buyer for his business, packed up Patrick and their few possessions and headed south across the Red River, into Texas. Their destination was Denton County where Hampton's sister Rosalind made her home.

Patrick's memory of what had happened in the store was vague and came back to him only in hazy patches. His father, wrapped up in his own grief, didn't understand the extent of the shock that that night had inflicted on the boy's young mind. When Patrick tried to ask him about that night, Hampton was unable to discuss it and brushed off the boy's questions. In his innocence, the boy accepted his father's wishes.

Hampton's sister Rosalind, a retired schoolteacher, had no children of her own. Her brother had only to ask her to take charge of his son's education and she was persuaded. She told her brother that he could not have given her anything that would make her happier than having that boy to nurture and educate. She moved Patrick into her own home and couldn't wait to get started teaching Patrick to read.

It was midsummer; Patrick was almost ten and had no formal schooling. Aunt Rosalind set about teaching him everything he would need to know to take his place in the schoolroom with his peers. She started with the alphabet and the sounds each letter could make. She was delighted that he could already add small sums of numbers in his head, a skill his father had taught him. He also enjoyed his free time, hunting in the local woods or fishing in a close-by swimming hole. His Aunt Rosalind gave him time free from his studies, knowing that part of being a boy was important too. But being the sole student under the tutelage of a skilled teacher, he learned quickly. By the time winter ended, the boy was reading aloud from *The Eclectic First Reader for Young Children* by W.H. McGuffey, pleasing his teacher and astounding his father. At the summer's end Rosalind was certain he could start to school at the same grade level as the other boys of his age.

Hampton Lanigan found a job with a large general store in Denton; content with no longer being the head man, he lived quietly. In August of 1860, Patrick was preparing to enrol in public school for the first time when his father died violently. The store manager, feeling Hampton was qualified by his frontier experience, had sent him to collect an overdue debt owed to the store by Hugo Harlan, a notorious local gambler. The official story the sheriff told was that Hampton got into an argument during a poker game with Harlan. The events according to Harlan and confirmed by witnesses, was that Hampton Lanigan became angry when he lost a big pot and accused Harlan of cheating. When Harlan objected, Lanigan went for his pistol which was in his inside coat pocket, but Harlan drew first and fired, hitting Lanigan in the heart.

Rosalind Lanigan told the sheriff that

she didn't believe one word of that story because her brother had never condoned gambling in any form and had never carried a gun. Patrick confirmed what his aunt said about the gun, maintaining that his father never owned even a handgun.

The sheriff explained that all he had to go on was what the witnesses confirmed and, though they were less than trustworthy, they were all he had. He confided to Rosalind that Hampton's employer confirmed sending him to collect the debt but he was too terrified of the gambler and his friends to testify.

The funeral was attended by only a few friends and colleagues of the retired teacher. Patrick stood at the graveside service dry-eyed, saying nothing. It was that night that he was first troubled by the voices.

He cried out in his sleep, waking his aunt. When she rushed to comfort him, he sobbed out, 'The old shaman was blaming me for my mother being killed.

He said I should have moved quickly and silently, like a true Indian, and killed that man before he could hurt my mother.' Rosalind, who had never heard the full story of Kiji's death, then heard for the first time that Patrick himself killed his mother's assailant with an axe. She held him in her arms and wept with him until he fell into an exhausted sleep.

After that night, the voices returned more and more frequently. Patrick soon learned to tolerate or drown them out with other things, on his own, without worrying his aunt. Sometimes, he heard his father's voice. At other times, it was the old shaman speaking in the old tongue. On occasion, he heard his mother's voice, sometimes scolding him and, at other times, crooning an Algonquin lullaby at bedtime. He concluded that he was insane but decided that as long as he didn't talk about the voices, no one else would know about it.

Denton, as most of Texas, was

untouched by the war's destruction except for the sacrifice of many young men to the losing cause. Patrick was too young for service, being only twelve when the war broke out. Knowing nothing of slavery before coming to Texas, he puzzled over the upheaval caused by the war. But since it was impossible not to be touched by the conflict, his Aunt Rosalind counselled him carefully, advising him not to get involved in any of the arguments over the war or slavery itself. She knew there were too many hotheads about for a young boy to talk too much. Also, she was horrified to learn that, in the county to the north, a citizen's court with no legal standing was hanging people merely suspected of being Yankee spies or sympathizers.

Patrick found a sure way to quiet the voices that hounded him. With money left him by his father, he bought a pistol, an old single-action .45. In his free time, he went into the woods near Rosalind's home and practiced shooting. He said nothing about this to anyone, his school mates or his aunt. Like so many things, he held it to himself.

As was to be expected, word got around among Patrick's fellow pupils that he was an Indian. As a result, some treated him with contempt, calling him half-breed. Some teased him but soon tired of it when he failed to react. Others didn't care one way or the other. But the situation came to a critical point one day during a game when Patrick accidentally knocked down another player. The boy got to his feet, snarling curses, and somewhere in the stream of invective, called Patrick 'a wagon-burner'. Patrick immediately flew into a rage and struck the boy in the face, breaking his nose and knocking him to the ground. He then leaned over the boy, grabbed him by the hair and yelled, 'Call me a wagon-burner again and I'll kill you.'

He turned to the bystanders and shouted, 'That goes for all of you.' His vehemence was frightening. 'Yes, by

God, I'm a Shawnee, and proud of it,' he yelled. 'If you don't like it, what are you going to do about it?'

He waited, fists clenched, lower jaw stuck out. There were no challengers.

From that day, the boys called him Shawnee and when they spoke that name, they did so with respect.

Patrick completed his formal schooling in the little schoolhouse a month after the war ended but he had little time to celebrate the war's end or his graduation. His Aunt Rosalind had been ailing for some months but she rarely spoke of it and carried on with her routine. One evening after supper, Aunt Rosalind sat beside him and told him she was fatally ill and there was nothing the doctor could do. When he started to despair, she dried his tears and told him not to grieve because teaching and caring for him had made her life complete. She smiled and confided in him that she would go to her maker a happy woman with a clear conscience. Patrick stayed at her side, seeing to her needs through her illness. He had to muster all the courage he could find to see her through those final days until the malignancy carried her away.

He arranged for the burial, settled up his aunt's affairs, sold her home and furnishings, packed up his few personal possessions, including his favourite books from Rosalind's library, and said goodbye to his friends. When asked where he was going, he answered only, 'Out there,' with a toss of his head. Late on an August afternoon in 1865, at the age of sixteen, he mounted his horse and, leading a loaded packmule, rode out of town.

The next morning, a friend of Hugo Harlan knocked on the sheriff's door while he was eating breakfast. The friend had found Harlan in his home, shot to death. The sheriff finished his breakfast and rode out to Harlan's two-room shack. After examining the body, he reasoned that whoever killed Hugo Harlan had hated the man intensely. The sheriff said the killer had prolonged his vengeance, first shooting the gambler in the legs, both arms, in the stomach and through the chest. Though Harlan had numerous enemies, the sheriff suspected Patrick Lanigan and sent out messages to the surrounding counties to be on the lookout for the sixteen-year-old. None of the sheriffs were able to find a young man by that name in his jurisdiction. The sheriff never solved the Hugo Harlan murder nor did his failure to do so cause him to lose any sleep.

1

In 1884, Texas was still in the post-war
agonies of change, going from an
agricultural slave-state to a rip-roaring
Mecca of beef and horse flesh. The
long-horns and wild mustangs that
freely roamed the prairies had been a
nuisance to those who farmed the land.
But after the Civil War, or the War of
Northern Aggression as it was known to
some, wild horses and longhorn cattle
went from nuisances to gold. The cattle
kings, taking advantage of the state's
open-range law, looked down on the
hard-working sod busters as nuisances
who ruined good grazing land by
ploughing it up and planting crops.
They also knew that the shortest
distance between two points was a
straight line. Therefore, with single-
minded purpose, they drove their great
masses of living merchandise across

corn fields, cotton crops or anything else that got in their way and there wasn't much a farmer could do about it. If one tried to interfere, he was likely to be shot. The law was stretched too thin to establish a presence in the state's vastness, much less protect the rights of all citizens. The only law at the margins of civilization was survival of the strongest, or the most ruthless.

On a Sunday afternoon in April of 1884, three men rode up the Rio Grande valley toward Eagle Pass. These were no ordinary men. Even the bravest drover or the most reckless wayfarer would have shuddered to meet the three. The leader was brutally ugly, his mutilated lower lip left most of his lower teeth exposed giving him a perpetual death's head grin. His eyes were grey and his stare was unsettling. One who put stock in the old saying that the eyes are windows to the soul, would know there was no soul behind those eyes, no sympathy, no love, nor any of the higher emotions. His gaze fell on everyone and everything the same: expressionless save for a trace of contempt. He wore a filthy and unkempt beard and long hair tied behind his head. At the point of an ugly scar on his forehead, the hair had turned white. Since his hair was rarely cut, a white streak extended back over his head in a continuous band.

Although the leader's two companions were less offensive to look upon, even the most casual observer would have avoided their company. The heavy brow of the taller of the two gave him a simian appearance. His uneven teeth were stained and his right incisor tooth was missing. When he took off his hat to mop the sweat, his mostly bald pate revealed scars of multiple encounters with fists, bottles and other instruments immediately available in barroom brawls. A fringe of greasy thin hair rimmed his bald head. He wore a perpetual sneer as if he detested the world surrounding him.

The shorter man had a generous

mop of unwashed hair and a week's growth of beard. His shoulders were wide and his arms were sinewy. His jaw hung loosely and he gazed upon the world through dull, muddy-brown eyes in seemingly mild surprise, as if seeing it for the first time.

Eagle Pass perched on the Rio Grande across from Ciudad Acuna in the state of Coahuila. None of the three was new to the town, but each had his reason for not visiting until now. The trio's leader had been in prison, another had been hiding from Texas law in Mexico and the third had gone to ground in an insignificant Texas town that few had heard of and fewer visited.

The leader spoke to the bald man. 'Manny, are you sure you know where the house is? I sure as hell ain't goin' to ride through Eagle Pass; wouldn't do for anyone to recognize one of us.'

The one called Manny replied, 'It's like I told you, Marsh. They put this neighbourhood together after you was sent off to Huntsville. I know 'xactly where Kincaid lives, right at the edge.'

'He damn well better be there,' the leader replied. 'After I finish my business with him, I want to ride straight on. I don't want to 'tract no more attention than I can help.'

The shorter man knitted his brow. 'You ain't planning to kill that Kincaid fellow, are you, Marsh, and get us in trouble again?'

Marsh turned in his saddle to glare at the speaker. 'Now, Al, don't you worry 'bout me and Kincaid. Him and me are goin' to reach an understanding.'

After that, the three rode on in silence.

At the trio's destination, Ward Kincaid and his six-year-old son were seated in the parlour, looking at a book filled with maps and artists' drawings of foreign lands. The boy sat in his father's lap as the father explained the pictures.

A movement outside the front window caught Ward Kincaid's eye and he looked up. When he saw the three men on horseback, he closed the book, lifted the boy to his feet and stood up. Kincaid was an impressive man, standing six feet two inches and, broad-shouldered. He had thick, black hair and wore a carefully trimmed moustache. He wore a white shirt open at the collar and dark trousers held up by suspenders.

He squinted his eyes against the setting sun so see the men's faces, then exclaimed, 'My God!'

He picked up the boy and hastened to the back of the house where his wife Betsy was ironing his freshly laundered shirts. She looked at her husband's face and said, 'Ward, what's wrong?'

'Keep little Brick back here and the two of you stay here out of sight,' Kincaid said softly. 'There's someone in front of the house that I don't want anywhere near either of you.'

'Ward, what is it?' she insisted, her blue eyes wide.

Ignoring her question, he said, 'Don't talk, stay quiet. Whatever you hear, don't come to the front of the house!'

He put the boy in her arms, turned

and strode back to the parlour.

He glanced through the window as he went to the door. He saw Marsh Kennebec, a pistol thrust into his belt, sauntering up the short walkway to the house, turning his head left and right to see if any neighbour might be watching. His two riding companions stayed in their saddles. The one called Manny began to roll a smoke.

Kincaid opened the door before Kennebec reached it and stood in the doorway. He stood three inches taller than the man with the mutilated lip. 'What do you want, Kennebec?' he asked.

Kennebec's grin grew more bizarre. 'Now what do you think I want, you holy mouth son-of-a-bitch?' he snarled.

'Don't make things worse, Kennebec,' Kincaid answered. 'You've served your time, and you're square with the State. You know they'll send you back if you violate the law in any way at all.'

'They gotta catch me first,' Kennebec hissed. 'But anyway, no law dogs are goin' to scare me off getting even with your uppity ass.'

Kennebec reached for the pistol in his belt.

Kincaid stepped forward and grabbed the gunman's arm. The two men grappled. Lurching back through the open doorway into the house, they sprawled on the floor. Kincaid used his greater weight to roll Kennebec over on his back and, leaning over him, delivered a hard right to his face.

Kennebec, half-blinded, rolled away, kicking at Kincaid's legs and still grasping the pistol. Kincaid fell to one knee but lurched toward the gunman. As Kincaid reached for him, Kennebec fired. The bullet hit the big man in the chest, knocking him to the floor. Kincaid cursed and reached for the gunman but Kennebec slithered away out of his reach.

There was a cry from the back of the house. 'Ward, what's happened?' Betsy called.

Kincaid started to shout a warning,

but his voice failed and he fell face down on the floor.

Betsy Kincaid ran into the room and screamed when she saw her husband on the floor, blood spreading under him. She knelt beside him, calling his name. Kennebec got to his feet and shoved the pistol back into his belt. He smiled at the terrified woman and said, 'Well now, ain't you the pretty one. I reckon I got some business with you as well.'

He lurched forward and seized her right arm with his left. He grabbed the neck of her dress and ripped it downward, exposing the undergarments beneath.

'Let's see what you got, you pretty little thing,' he snarled.

Betsy Kincaid realized what the man was after and utter revulsion replaced her horror. Kennebec read her expression, one he had been seeing practically all his life. Rage pushed thoughts of rape from his mind. He threw her against the wall and pulled the pistol from his belt, and screamed, 'Look at me like that, will you, bitch?' He fired point blank into her chest. 'How do you like that?'

She fell back against the wall, mouth agape. Her knees buckled and she sagged to a sitting position, her back against the wall, her head falling forward.

He turned and strode out the door.

Little Brick ran into the room. His mother and father were motionless amid welters of blood. He ran to the open door and looked out at the man who had just killed his parents.

Brick's dog Cochise, a big, friendly mixed-breed retriever, had been hunting alone in the fields behind the house. Attracted by the horses and activity, he trotted up into the yard as Kennebec left the house. The dog, who had never met a stranger, trotted up to Kennebec, expecting a pat on the head. Instead, Kennebec drew his pistol and fired. The dog yelped and fell.

The rider called Al blurted, 'Hell's fire, Marsh! What you do that for?'

Kennebec climbed into his saddle and said to his stunned companions, 'I never did like dogs. 'Sides, he coulda bit me. What the hell difference does it make? Let's ride!'

The three men kicked their mounts into a gallop and swiftly rode away.

A neighbour had been breaking ground for his vegetable garden behind his house when he heard the shots. He ran from behind his house in time to see the three men ride away to the north. He saw Brick Kincaid in the front yard of his house kneeling by something on the ground and ran to him.

The boy sat quietly by the dead dog, his face expressionless. The neighbour cried out, 'Brick, what in the world has happened here?' The boy looked at him with dry eyes but didn't answer.

2

Hattie was sleeping soundly and, since he detested goodbyes, Shawnee Lanigan slipped out of bed quietly and gathered up his boots, gun belt and clothes. Since he had to take a leak something terrible, he thought it best to ease out of the hotel room with his clothes in his hands and slip down to the toilet, relieve himself and get dressed there.

His plan worked until he almost reached the toilet at the end of the hall. A door to one of the rooms opened and a lady emerged, took one look at Shawnee and said, with lips curled into a sneer, 'Another one of you sons-a-bitches sneakin' out!'

Shawnee gave her an indignant look, or at least, with as much indignation as he could muster while barefooted and mostly naked. He opened the toilet door and dodged in, urinated with a sigh of relief, slipped into his clothes, pushed back his black hair with one hand and put on his black, high-crowned hat. He took the back stairs out to the rear of the hotel and walked down the alley about half a block, cut between a couple of buildings and emerged on the boardwalk. Then he headed for Flossie's Place.

An astute observer would not call Shawnee Lanigan handsome. As looks go, he was inoffensive, six feet in height, watched the world through dark-brown eyes, and had a strong chin and prominent cheekbones. However, he held a natural attraction for the ladies. It was perhaps because Shawnee liked the ladies themselves. Every time he met someone new, his excitement was contagious. The thrill of the unknown, of exploration and discovery animated him to new heights of affection.

At Flossie's Place, Shawnee pushed open the door and the aroma of frying bacon washed over him, making his mouth water. He took a chair at an unoccupied table and no sooner had his butt hit the chair than Flossie herself put down a big mug of coffee right in front of him.

'Not a moment too soon, milady,' he said, grinning up at Flossie's florid face set atop Flossie's formidable body.

Flossie ignored the put-on charm and asked in her gravely, no-nonsense voice, 'What'll you have this morning, you shiftless bum?'

'Flossie!' Shawnee exclaimed. 'You cut me to the quick. Here I am, one of your most ardent admirers looking for a smile from your sweet face to give me courage to face the day.' He gave her his best hang-dog face. 'And you cut me like a bastard stepchild.'

'You got the money to pay for breakfast, Shawnee?' she asked, gazing at him askance.

'You cut me again!' he said, sticking out his lower lip. 'I assure you I have sufficient funds.'

She put her hands on her hips and

fixed him with a silent stare. Giving in to her relentless gaze, he reached into his right-hand pants' pocket, pulled out forty-five cents and plunked it down on the table. Flossie reached down, took thirty-five cents of it and said, 'One special coming up,' and walked away.

Considering his options, Shawnee soon concluded that he had only one, to find a job. He picked up his last ten cents from the table and put it back in his pants' pocket. He reviewed his expenditures of late, including frolicking with the soiled doves at Madam Celeste's House of Earthly Delights and extended poker games with the likes of Bum McReedy, Wall-Eye Brewster and Trace-Chain Stokes.

Flossie brought Shawnee's breakfast and unceremoniously put it down in front of him without speaking. It was Flossie's special; three fried eggs, a fried ham steak swimming in red-eye gravy, grits and four biscuits. Shawnee considered his thirty-five cents a sound investment.

Shawnee was mopping up the last of the red-eye gravy with his last biscuit when Emory Horn, Sheriff of Rio County, opened the front door. He saw Shawnee and strode over, pulled back a chair from the table and spun it around. He sat down with his elbows resting on the chair back, indicating he wasn't there to eat but to do business. The sheriff was in his fifties, grey-haired but still fit. His eyes were pale blue and carried in them a hint of world-weariness.

'Shawnee,' he said in his usual no-nonsense manner, 'I'm glad I saw you. I have a telegraph message at the office from a fellow named Bryson over in Eagle Pass. I think he's got a job of work for you.'

'Know what kind of job, Sheriff?' Shawnee asked, feeling a sense of relief.

'No, not exactly,' came the answer. The sheriff glanced around to make certain no one was listening in on the conversation. 'But I reckon it's getting even with someone or maybe bringing some murdering bastard to the bar of justice.'

'How do you figure that?'

'I've known Brick Bryson for 'bout thirty years,' the sheriff answered. 'I know he lost his daughter and his son-in-law not too long ago; shot down in cold blood in their own home. My bet is he's going to want you to find the fellow who did it and bring him back to Eagle Pass for trial or maybe just kill 'im. Maybe he's heard about that Injun blood of yours and he figures you can track down anybody.'

'Well, the least I can do is go talk to the man,' Shawnee said.

'Good!' the sheriff said. 'It'll keep you out of my hair for a few days anyway. Let's go over to the jail and I'll give you the message.'

The two men left the café and headed toward the jail at a casual pace. They were chatting pleasantly when they were interrupted by a shout. 'Shawnee Lanigan, you son of a bitch!'

Shawnee turned to see Jacob Mason,

a large, thick-necked man, striding toward him, his face glowing red with rage. That florid face atop that massive body would have badly frightened an ordinary man.

'Lanigan, you dirty bastard,' he rasped. 'You been bothering my girl and I'm gonna whup yer ass!'

'Your girl?' Shawnee responded with a chuckle. 'You talking about Hattie Sanford?'

The sheriff stopped where he was and leaned against the building behind him to watch the show.

Mason cautioned the sheriff. 'Now you stay out of this, Sheriff. This is between me and this highbinder, this thief in the night, this molester of decent females.'

The sheriff nodded his assent and looked mildly amused.

'You got anything to say, Lanigan?' Mason roared.

'Molesting?' Shawnee replied, enunciating each syllable carefully. 'All I got to say is with all the whoopin' and hollarin' sweet Hattie was doin', my molestin' techniques must be pretty good.'

With a roar, Mason charged Shawnee, arms waving.

Shawnee was smaller than his assailant but his lithe physique gave him the advantage of speed and agility. He sidestepped the bigger man's headlong rush, ducked under a wildly swinging right arm and jabbed Mason in the ribs as he roared by. Mason stumbled to a stop and turned to look at Shawnee with a flicker of bewilderment crossing his face. He raised his hands to a semblance of a boxing fighter's position and stepped in more cautiously. Shawnee threw a left jab to the big man's nose and danced backward out of reach. Mason's eyes watered as he tried to size up his smaller but quicker opponent. He rushed again, this time holding off on his ineffectual punching but with hands extended toward Shawnee, grabbing at the smaller man with both arms. Once again, Shawnee ducked and threw a right uppercut to Mason's crotch. Mason let out a grunt and bent over. When he did, Shawnee brought his right knee up into the big man's face. The impact straightened up Mason and, with a blank expression on his face, he fell backward to the boardwalk. He lay motionless, blood pouring from his distorted nose.

The sheriff asked, 'Are you finished here, Lanigan?'

'Looks like it, Sheriff,' Shawnee replied.

Both men started once again toward the jail.

'Sheriff!' a feminine voice cried. 'Aren't you going to arrest that man?' The lady was pointing at Shawnee with her parasol.

The sheriff stopped and answered, 'Why would I do that?'

The lady was indignant. 'Because he beat up that man lying there and left him bloody and unconscious, right here in the public street.'

The sheriff looked at Mason who was

starting to stir and groan.

'Looks like self-inflicted wounds to me, ma'am,' the sheriff replied, tipping his hat and continuing on his course.

At the jail, Sheriff Horn pulled the message out of his desk drawer and handed it to Shawnee.

Reading over it, Shawnee said, 'Well, I reckon I'll be leaving in the morning early to see what Mr Bryson has to say. By the way, Sheriff, I'm down to ten cents and it won't get me all the way to Eagle Pass. Now I can do without food, but my horse is used to eating on a regular basis. You reckon you might see your way clear to loan me a few dollars?'

'Shawnee,' the sheriff said, 'you beat any damned thing I ever saw. What happened to the money you made on that last job of yours? I happen to know there was enough in that payoff to support a normal family for a year.'

'Well,' Shawnee said slowly, 'I ran into some unexpected expenses and there are folks depending on me.'

'Yeah, sure,' the sheriff mumbled. 'A dozen bartenders and half the whores in Rio County.'

After very little more conversation, the sheriff handed Shawnee a ten-dollar bill and said, between clenched teeth, 'Before you play a hand of poker, before you buy a damned drink, before you walk into a whorehouse and drop your britches, you pay the county back! You understand?'

Shawnee looked hurt. 'Sheriff, don't you trust me? You cut me to the quick!'

After finishing his business with Sheriff Horn, Shawnee sauntered to the stable where he had boarded his brown-and-white paint horse Candy and settled up with the stable manager. He saddled up Candy, and rode to his boarding house where he picked up his Colt Model 1878, Frontier double-action .44–40, his Winchester .38–40 lever-action rifle, his hunting knife and his war bag. On the way out of town, he filled two bags with water, bought some oats for

Candy and some air-tights for his own consumption, got everything stowed and nudged Candy to a gentle lope, leaving town heading northwest along the river.

3

Two days after leaving home Shawnee guided Candy into the midst of Eagle Pass and up to the jail. There he inquired as to the whereabouts of Brick Bryson and obtained directions.

Brick Bryson's hair was grey, the years were etched deeply in his face but he moved with strength and the authority of a younger man, one accustomed to leadership. He offered Shawnee his hand and asked him to come into his office at the rear of his house. The room was sparsely furnished but comfortable, and loaded bookshelves covered two walls. Bryson sat behind a massive mahogany desk in a large leather-covered swivel chair. Shawnee sat in front of the desk in a comfortable guest chair. Bryson offered him a drink.

'No sir, but thanks anyway,' Shawnee said. 'I never drink when I'm talking business and I never talk business when I'm drinking.'

Bryson smiled. 'A wise policy, Mr Lanigan,' he said. 'Though I am surprised. From what I've heard about you, you are . . . well . . . a rough and tumble sort of person; one who defies not only society's conventions but the law as well.'

Shawnee allowed himself the hint of a smile and said, 'What you have heard is pretty close to the mark, Mr Bryson. However, I try to stay within the law when possible. But too many people I deal with have no code of conduct. When you try to keep a code of chivalry when dealing with people who have no morals, no religion and no personal values other than personal gain or just staying alive, it puts a decent man at a distinct disadvantage.'

Bryson raised an eyebrow during Shawnee's explanation. 'Again you surprise me. Chivalry? Are you an educated man, Mr Lanigan?'

'Not in any formal sense, sir,'

Shawnee responded. 'But the whole world is at your fingertips if you can read.'

Bryson smiled and nodded. 'You are a man of many parts, Mr Lanigan,' he said. 'But let us get to the matter at hand.'

Bryson rose from his chair, went to the mantel over the fireplace and picked up a framed photograph. He looked at it with affection and handed it to Shawnee. 'This is a portrait of my daughter made just before her marriage. My wife died right after Betsy was born. So I had a nurse for Betsy, to take care of her while I worked. There were two parts to my life, Mr Lanigan: my work and Betsy. I loved her more than words can tell and I made sure she had the best teachers, the best clothes; the best that money could buy. She was beautiful, gracious and bright, everything a woman should be. She fell in love with Ward Kincaid, one of the best men you would ever hope to know, and as far as I was concerned, she couldn't have done better anywhere. They adored one another and Betsy was happy. But then the state let Marsh Kennebec out of prison, something they never should have done. He should have stayed in that hole until he rotted and the maggots made a meal of him. He came here within days of getting out of prison. He went to Ward and Betsy's house and he killed both of them.'

The old man turned away from Shawnee. He took out a handkerchief and wiped at his face. After a few moments he turned back around.

'By the grace of God,' he went on, 'Ward had the boy hide when he saw who was walking up to the door. If he had not, I'm convinced Kennebec would have killed him, too. Little Brick was hiding but he could hear the whole thing. That's how we know it was Kennebec. Little Brick remembered everything his father said to that bastard. And he heard the shots, his mother screaming. He came out of his hiding-place and found his mother and father dead in the parlour. He looked out the front door in time to see that monster shoot his dog. Then Kennebec got on his horse and rode away. There were two men with him. We know who they are, too.'

Bryson went to the door, opened it and called, 'Little Brick.'

Lanigan heard the boy answer and almost immediately the child appeared at the door.

'You called, Grandfather?' he asked.

'Yes, I did, Brick. I want you to meet someone,' the old man replied.

The boy walked in and stood before Lanigan. Lanigan got to his feet and extended his hand.

Bryson said, 'Brick, this is Mr Shawnee Lanigan. He's a tracker.'

The boy shook Shawnee's hand vigorously. 'Are you an Indian?' he asked.

'About one quarter, son,' Shawnee answered. 'My mother was half Shawnee from up in the territory. I got enough Injun blood in me to let me 'sniff out men just a like a bloodhound.'

'Good! I am very happy to make your acquaintance, sir!' the boy exclaimed.

'Mr Lanigan wants to know what Marsh Kennebec looks like, Brick,' Bryson said. 'Can you tell him?'

'Yes sir, I can,' the boy answered without emotion. He turned to Shawnee. 'He's not a little man or what you'd call a big man. He's close to your size but his arms are longer like a gorilla's.'

The boy walked with his arms held out slightly from his body and swayed like a monkey walking on his hind legs.

'He's bad ugly and his lower teeth on the left side show cause something is wrong with his lower lip,' the boy continued. 'He has long dark hair going grey, and he keeps it pulled back and fastened like a woman's so it looks like a horse's tail. And right down the middle, starting in front, it's already gone white.'

The boy pointed to his own forehead and moved his finger back. 'From here

45

to the back of his head, there's a white streak, kind of like a skunk.'

'That's one heck of a good description, Brick,' Shawnee said. 'You know how to keep your eyes open. Whenever I run up on that rascal, I sure won't have any trouble recognizing him.'

Something hard flickered in the boy's eyes. 'Good luck to you, Mr Lanigan. I shall look forward to your return,' he said in an almost emotionless voice.

'Thank you, Brick,' the old man said. 'You can go back to your studies now.'

The boy said to Shawnee, 'Pleased to have met you, sir. Goodbye.' He started to turn but stopped. 'Mr Lanigan,' he said. 'Just before you kill him, I want Kennebec to know why he's dying, for killing my parents and Cochise, my dog. Can you tell him that?'

'I can guarantee it,' Shawnee said.

The boy allowed himself a grim smile, then walked out.

Shawnee stared at the closed door, frowning. 'He sure is a serious young fellow, isn't he?'

'Yes, a little too serious,' the grandfather answered. 'He hasn't shed a tear. Not a tear. He's acted and talked that way since his parents died. It isn't normal and I'm worried sick about it. I don't want the boy to grow up with this thing on his mind and holding it all in and thinking about revenge. It can cause a cancer on a man's soul and finally eat him up. I want to be able to tell him Kennebec has gone to his judgement and is roasting in hell. Then maybe he can work on being a little boy again.'

Bryson sat down and looked at Shawnee with one eyebrow raised. 'Want the job?'

Shawnee looked at the door the boy had gone through. 'I reckon I do, Mr Bryson.'

'What's your fee?' Bryson asked.

'Expenses and one thousand dollars for bringing back Kennebec or his scalp,' Shawnee said. 'If the job requires me to kill anyone besides Kennebec, it's two hundred and fifty for each of them.'

'Fair enough!' the old man said. He opened a folder on the desk and wrote a cheque.

'Here's two hundred dollars' advance to cover expenses. You can talk to the county sheriff for details on those two men who rode with Kennebec. He's expecting you.'

Shawnee got to his feet, picked up the cheque and shook hands with Bryson.

'I'll keep you posted by telegraph whenever I can without tipping my hand,' he said. 'If you go for more than two weeks without hearing from me, you can figure I leaned into a bullet and you're out two hundred dollars.'

'I would be very surprised if that happens, Mr Lanigan,' Bryson said, smiling. 'But if it does, we'll say a prayer for you in church.'

'Well that's mighty good of you, sir. If I'm roasting on a fiery spit down in hell and I feel a cool breeze giving me a few moments of relief, I'll know you've said that prayer.'

4

While Shawnee sat in front of his desk drinking coffee from a tin cup, Sheriff Jose de la Torre filled him in on the details. 'The reason Marsh Kennebec went to prison in the first place was Ward Kincaid interrupted him during an attempted rape of a *niña*. Kincaid gave him a beating and turned him over to the law. After the judge passed sentence on him, Kennebec swore he'd get even with Ward Kincaid. During all those years in prison, his hate for Ward Kincaid must have festered like a boil on his soul. Kennebec was evil to his very bone when he went to prison, but when he came out, even *El Diablo* would not claim him.'

'How old was the girl?' Shawnee asked.

'Only nine years,' de la Torre answered with a look of disgust, then he smoothed back the head of hair that no longer was there. 'She was the child of parents who did not watch her closely enough.'

He got up and went to a map on the wall. 'After the Kincaids were killed, and we could not find Kennebec, I did some backtracking. I found out Kennebec was travelling with two men, Manny Cephus and Alfred Tutt. Cephus had met Kennebec with a horse when he walked out the prison gate. Sometime later they met up with Tutt, another ex-convict. They went into Mexico. Cephus and Tutt were still riding with Kennebec when he killed the Kincaids. Both of them were from this part of the country. Cephus came from a little place north of San Felipe del Rio called Juno, and Tutt is from somewhere outside Fort Stockton. It was believed the three originally teamed up for mischief after meeting in Piedras Negras.'

'You went after them?'

'Yes. When we found out about the Kincaids they had a head start of about two hours on us. You know this country, Lanigan. There's a thousand places to hide, not counting the most convenient one, Mexico. The posse searched for three days. After that, I looked for them with just my men for another week. We could never get a lead on them. I suspect if they didn't go back into Mexico, they went on up toward San Felipe. We never could pick up a thing. Anyone who knew where they were heading was one of their friends or just too afraid to talk.'

'That's where I have the advantage, Sheriff,' Shawnee said. 'A posse might scare too many people but just one ordinary-lookin' cowhand just might find some answers.'

'Good point, Lanigan,' de la Torre agreed. 'You can go where I can't.' He handed Shawnee two sheets of paper. 'Here are the descriptions of Tutt and Cephus according to their prison records.'

'Where is this place called Juno?'

'It's north of San Felipe del Rio. I

believe it's on the Rio Diablo.'

'Thanks,' Shawnee said, getting to his feet and heading for the door.

'I wish you luck,' de la Torre said. 'And Lanigan . . . '

Shawnee stopped in the door and turned around.

'*Cuidado!*'[1]

★ ★ ★

'Who in the hell are you to be asking about people like that?' the marshal blurted.

Shawnee had spent three days making the fifty-mile trip up the river to San Felipe del Rio without problems other than mosquitoes and other varmints. He had slept well on the trail and, when he arrived, he was in a good mood. That changed after he met the sheriff.

Shawnee was momentarily taken aback by the man's hostility. 'I'm doing

_____

[1] Take care!

a favour for a friend,' he said. 'Sheriff de la Torre said you would be glad to help.'

'Oh he did, did he?' the sheriff asked with a malicious grin. The sheriff stared at Shawnee's cheekbones and dark hair and said, 'You look like an Injun yourself. You and the greaser must be old friends.'

Shawnee felt the heat spread over his face at the insulting words. His first impulse was to punch the grin off that ugly face, but he swallowed hard instead.

'So you haven't seen or heard anything about these three men?' Shawnee asked.

The sheriff looked up at him and said, 'I didn't say that.'

Shawnee replied, 'Oh? They friends of yours?'

The sheriff sprang to his feet. 'Look, you Goddamned bounty huntin' wagon-burner, I don't need your insults! Now get your ass out of this office before I lock it up!'

Shawnee felt anger in every pore of his body. He paused, getting a grip on his emotions, stiffly got to his feet, smiled thinly, tipped his hat and said, 'Thanks for your help, Sheriff,' as he walked out the door.

In the street, Shawnee looked both ways, taking in the names of the establishments and giving himself time to calm down. There was a saloon nearby but an adobe cantina at the end of the street was of more interest. He knew the saloon would be populated with Anglos who might well share the sheriff's undisguised contempt for non-Anglo-Saxons, so he reasoned he might find a friendlier ear at the cantina. He climbed aboard Candy for the short trip down the street.

Shawnee strode into the cantina with a confident air. The place smelled of beer and tobacco smoke. He drew a few stares but the drinkers quickly returned to their conversations and their drinks. Shawnee leaned against the bar, tilted his hat back and said, '*Cerveza.*'

The bartender eyed Shawnee suspiciously but drew a beer and set it in front of him. Shawnee put twenty-five cents down on the bar, took a sip of the beer and made a wry face.

'You got a horse out back you get this stuff out of?' Shawnee asked.

The bartender looked at Shawnee with a smirk as he laid twenty cents on the bar. 'What do you want for five cents, señor, French wine?'

'Not only does the beer taste second hand, I've gotta put up with a wise-ass bartender,' Shawnee snorted.

The bartender leaned over the bar and looked at Shawnee's feet. 'Your feet aren't nailed to the floor, my Anglo friend,' he said.

'Is it you've got all the customers you want, or is it you just don't like Anglos?' Shawnee growled, squinting at the bartender.

The bartender threw up his hands in a gesture of helplessness. 'It's the Anglos,' he said. 'If we don't watch out, they're going to take over.'

Shawnee and the bartender burst out laughing at the same time. The other patrons, who had been watching the exchange in anticipation of a brawl, joined in the laughter.

Shawnee held out his hand and said, 'I'm Shawnee Lanigan. I ain't from around here.'

The bartender took the hand and shook it firmly. 'I am Chuy Esperanza. And I know you are not from here. A local Anglo would not come in this place.'

Shawnee nodded. 'I suppose you are wondering why I came in here?'

'*Sí*, I wonder a bit. Could be you are looking for information?' Chuy responded.

'You have that right,' Shawnee said, putting a five-dollar coin on the bar. Chuy eyed the coin and asked, 'You are looking for some Anglo bad men?'

Shawnee nodded.

Chuy picked up the coin and put it in his pocket. 'I'm a poor man,' he said. 'I sell information on Anglo bad men very cheaply.'

'You know the marshal?' Shawnee asked.

'Oh yes, we all know him well,' Chuy responded, then turned his head and spat. Shawnee watched the gesture and nodded. 'I kinda feel the same way myself after trying to talk to the man. Have you any idea why he threatened to lock me up?'

'Sure,' the bartender said. 'As a lawman, he can't collect any reward placed on the heads of the outlaws if he catches them himself. So when he catches one, he has his son-in-law pretend to have caught him and collect the reward.'

Shawnee threw back his head and laughed. 'Well, that's a relief to know. At least him not liking me was nothing personal. It was strictly business.'

Chuy joined Shawnee in his laughter and pulled another beer. 'You have names?' he asked.

'Yes, I do,' Shawnee replied. 'Marsh Kennebec, Manny Cephus and Alfred Tutt. Any of them sound familiar?'

'*Sí*, they are familiar,' Chuy answered. 'And if I was not a grown man, I would weep in fear at the mention of those names. They are bad men. If you seek those three, *vaya con Dios*, my friend.'

'Have they been here?' Shawnee asked.

'I have not seen them myself.' Chuy motioned to a man seated at a table. The man got up and walked toward them. 'But buy my friend, Sinecio, a drink and he might be helpful.'

Chuy, speaking in Spanish, asked Sinecio what he wanted to drink and added that the Anglo was buying.

Sinecio ordered tequila, looked at Shawnee and said, '*Muchas gracias.*'

Chuy asked the man if he had seen any of the three men Shawnee named. Sinecio looked unhappy and tossed down his shot of tequila without blinking. Then he began to answer in Spanish and Chuy interpreted.

'He works at a large hacienda to the north of town a few miles. He says three men stopped and spent the night;

the owner is a friend of one of them. He saw them come from the house the next morning, they talked, said *adios* to one another and rode away. He understands some English but pretends not to and he had the impression each was going his own way. It was later in the day when he learned who the men were and it frightened him. He is still afraid.'

'They didn't know he overheard them?' Shawnee asked and Chuy translated.

'No. He gave no sign. He says sometimes it pays to be a dumb Mexican,' Chuy quoted Sinecio with a smile.

'I wonder if Kennebec's friends were heading for their homes,' Shawnee mused out loud. 'If so, it might pay to track one of them down to find out where Kennebec went.'

'You know where these men live?' Chuy asked.

'Sort of, at least where they started from. I suppose that's where I'll try first,' Shawnee replied. 'How do I find a place called Juno?'

Chuy said, 'Follow the Rio Grande

northwest from here, you will come upon the Rio Diablo. Follow the Rio Diablo north to where it forks with Ricardo Creek. Juno is just north of the fork.' Chuy wiped at the bar with a rag and added, 'If you live, come back and say hello, *por favor*?'

'I'll do that,' Shawnee smiled grimly as he headed for the door.

When Shawnee rode by the sheriff's office on his way out of town, the sheriff was on the boardwalk talking to a deputy. When the sheriff looked up and glared at him, Shawnee touched the brim of his hat in greeting and, smiling broadly, said, 'Thanks for your help, Sheriff.'

'That ought to pique his curiosity,' Shawnee said to Candy as he spurred her to a lope.

*   *   *

The road to Juno along the Rio Diablo was no different from all rides through that rugged land. There were the usual coyotes, an occasional wild goat, and lizards and snakes sometimes disturbed by Candy's hoofs. It was a barren part of the world where the sparse vegetation clung to life precariously. He saw a few herds of goat, the only meat animal that could glean a living from the harsh land. The Rio Diablo carried little water at that time of year and only cactus and mesquite trees broke the monotony of the land. An occasional dry breeze stirred up dust devils from the arid soil.

He stuck to the west bank of the river till he reached the fork with the even dryer Ricardo Creek. North of the fork, he saw Juno. The settlement, which was not on Shawnee's map, consisted of a general store which had been built from the local stone, a stable and a small café. He pulled into the stable to water Candy and found an elderly man puttering around, cleaning up.

Shawnee dismounted, stretched his back and spoke to the stableman.

'Howdy. My name's Shawnee Lanigan. Can I leave my mount here in the shade while I get something to eat?'

'Sure, you can leave her. I'll feed her for two bits,' the old man said.

'Fair enough,' Shawnee answered. 'That café over there open?'

'Oh yeah, it's open.'

'I reckon I'll go over there and get me a hot meal,' Shawnee said.

'That's good, long as you like *frijoles* and beer,' the old man responded.

'Beans and beer?' Shawnee asked in surprise. 'Is that it?'

'That's it.'

'Well, that meal gives you something to do the rest of the day,' Shawnee mused.

The café was small and smelled of beans cooking. Shawnee sat down at a table and asked what was on the menu.

'You don't know?' the proprietor, asked in a European accent.

'This is my first time here,' Shawnee answered.

'We have *frijoles* and *tortillas*.'

'What else?'

'Beer.'

'I'll tell you what,' Shawnee said, 'I'll have *frijoles* and beer.'

'*Frijoles* and beer, coming up,' the man said cheerily. 'Tortillas on the side.'

Shawnee had to admit the beans were hot and tasty and the beer was cool. As he ate, the proprietor walked over to his table.

The little man asked in his heavy accent, 'I haven't seen you before; passing through?'

'You might say that. I'm Shawnee Lanigan. I'm looking for someone who used to live around here.'

'I'm Henry Stein,' the man said. 'I know all the people who live here.'

'Do you know Manny Cephus?' Shawnee asked.

The smile faded from Stein's face and he stood up.

'You a friend of his?' Stein asked in a flat tone.

'No, I'm not,' Shawnee replied. 'In fact, I never met the man. I just need to get some information from him.'

Stein looked relieved. 'I know this man. He is not a good man.'

'Sit down, Mr Stein,' Shawnee invited. 'Tell me about Cephus.'

Stein sat down, leaned forward and spoke in a soft voice. 'Manfred Cephus was born in these parts, actually before this town existed. His family home is north about six miles. His sister lives in the old family home and comes here every once in a while for supplies. I did not know him when he was a child but I understand he was a bad seed from the time he could walk, and he has been in prison for robbery and other things. People here are frightened of him.'

'Is he here now?'

'I don't know,' Stein said, shaking his head. 'I have not seen him. You might ask the Ansleys at the general store. They hear a great deal. And the Cephus girl buys supplies there.'

Shawnee finished the last of his beans, chewed the last tortilla and washed it down with the last of the beer. 'Thanks, Mr Stein. You have been very helpful.'

'Are you looking to kill this man or arrest him?' Stein asked with a note of hope in his voice.

'Whatever I have to do.'

'May God hold you in his hand, Mr Lanigan,' Stein said.

Shawnee walked over to the general store and went in. A lady's voice called from the back of the room, 'Can I help you, mister?'

'I reckon you can if you are Mrs Ansley,' he answered.

'That's me, stranger,' the lady answered, walking to the front of the store. 'What can I do for you?'

'I'm looking for information, ma'am,' Shawnee responded. 'I'm trying to track down Manny Cephus.'

'You the law?' she asked.

'Nope. Just somebody hired to do a job. Can you help me?'

'If you're going to send that trashy bastard to hell, I'll be glad to help,' Mrs Ansley said with a chuckle. 'What do you want to know?'

Shawnee said, 'I understand his sister comes in here for supplies; she been in lately?'

'That would be Beryl,' the lady said. 'And yes, she's been in lately. She has an old mule she hitches up to a wagon and drives in. I'd guess it was about a week ago she came in here and loaded up pretty good.'

'She buy an unusual amount of goods?'

'Yep. Usually she spends about five dollars. This time she spent a little over ten. It was unusual, that's why I remember.'

'Sounds like maybe she was feeding somebody other than herself,' Shawnee said.

'That's the way I figured it,' Mrs Ansley responded. 'I thought at the time she found herself a man, though God help the poor pilgrim who'd want to romance *her*,' she added, grimacing. 'It didn't occur to me her brother might be back. I'se hoping he was dead and buried in some boot hill someplace.'

'I understand he's overdue for retirement,' Shawnee said.

'You're damned right he is,' the lady spat. 'I reckon the almighty must be testin' our faith letting that piece of trash run around breathing.'

Shawnee got detailed instructions from the storekeeper as to how to find the Cephus home place and went back to the stable. It was getting late in the day so he decided to get some sleep and set out in the morning. The stable man let him pitch his bedroll in a fairly clean corner of the stable for twenty-five cents. Shawnee saw to his horse, then bedded down himself. He slept soundly during the night, as he usually did when tracking someone. The voices were quiet.

The next morning, he woke with the sun. Deciding he didn't want *frijoles* and beer for breakfast, he made his own coffee and ate some tinned food from his own gear. The little town was starting to stir when he rode out along the north road.

The road wasn't much more than a trail through the hills but it was easy to follow. He topped a hill and there on the other side of a draw was the Cephus home place as it had been described. It wasn't much of a home place, being a small cabin built with local rock, a privy and a shed in back and what looked like a well in front of the house. Smoke drifted from the chimney but no one was in sight.

Shawnee dismounted, led Candy back to where she would be hidden from the house, grounded the reins so she'd stay put and, taking his spyglass from his saddlebag, crept back to a vantage point where he could observe the place at leisure. Through a window, he glimpsed occasional movement. Two animals stood in the shed, a mule and a horse. A few chickens gleaned a poor living from the yard around the house.

Suddenly, there was a shot and a slug whizzed past his head, knocking bark off a nearby post oak. Shawnee scrambled around to get something between himself and the direction from which the shot had come. As he did, another shot came from the house and kicked up dirt by his head.

He was caught in a crossfire!

5

Shawnee cursed his short sightedness and his complacency. His rifle was in its scabbard on his saddle and Candy was several yards away. He scuttled backward crablike to find a lower place to hide. Another shot from the cabin kicked a sharp rock into his cheek below his right eye.

How did they know I was here? Shawnee wondered. *One of them must have seen me come up the road.*

He crawled into a shallow wash where he was invisible to both shooters for the time being. He tried to remember the terrain surrounding him and the horse. He would have to take a desperate chance to get his rifle because he had no hope of taking on two riflemen with a six-shooter. He reasoned that if Manny Cephus and his sister were shooting, neither of them was on horseback because two animals were in the shed. He took his Colt from its holster and loaded the sixth chamber. He had perhaps two dozen rounds in his cartridge belt but only one weapon. Reloading the pistol in a pitched battle would make him vulnerable to a rush attack.

Shawnee felt blood dripping off his chin. He took his bandanna from around his neck and dabbed at it. He had forgotten about the rock hitting his cheek. That one was too close! He was getting careless, he thought; too much whiskey and too much frolicking with the girls.

He took stock of his situation. Only a bold move could get him out of this spot. The ground behind him sloped downward. If he could reach the bottom of the hill, he had some cover in the scrub brush and small oaks growing on both sides of the road. If he could get to the bottom undetected, he might be able to work his way past the house and approach it from the other side. It would be a long and arduous process but he saw no other way of escaping from the trap he had let himself fall into.

He started crawling down the slope.

* * *

Two hours had passed since he started crawling. The cabin was just opposite him across the road. His hands and knees were bloody and covered with dirt. In another hundred yards he could try to cross the road. He remembered the road dropped off a hill behind the house and disappeared for a short distance. If he could get there, he could dash across the road unobserved from the hill he had left. He had heard nothing from Cephus or his sister, no shouts, no calls, no whistles. They were savvy enough to know, since they didn't know where he was, that they should make no sound that would disclose their locations to him.

Shawnee was now a good distance

beyond the house and he crawled toward the road. He was right! After the road passed in front of the cabin it went on for perhaps seventy-five yards, then dropped steeply down the backside of the hill. He approached the road cautiously and, before giving up his brushy cover, stopped and carefully observed the area above him. He saw no movement.

He crawled to the edge of the road, leaped to his feet and dashed across the narrow tracks to the brush on the other side. No shots came and there was no movement above. He moved quickly in a crouch through the brush and the small oaks until he was no longer visible from the road. He then started back toward the cabin, still moving in a crouch. Reaching the slope, he paused to wipe the clotted blood and dirt from his hands. He pulled his Colt from its holster and started up the slope. At the top, he fell to his stomach and watched the cabin. No one was visible outside the cabin nor could he see movement through the windows. Then he saw movement from the hill above the house. Beryl Cephus was leading Candy down the hill. She had apparently given up the search for him and was taking his horse, his rifle and his other equipment back to the cabin. Shawnee waited until she reached level ground before moving up to the outbuildings behind the cabin. He reached the shed sheltering the horses and stopped.

The cabin's back door opened and a man came out. Shawnee recognized the narrow eyes and battered nose. It was Manny Cephus. Cephus moved to the shed, picked up a bridle and started to put it on his horse. Hidden from Beryl Cephus by the cabin, Shawnee edged to the front of the shed and as Manny was putting the bridle on the horse, Shawnee stepped up behind him, stuck the Colt in the small of Manny's back and said, 'Don't move and stay quiet, you son-of-a-bitch, or I'll kill you.'

Manny gasped and stiffened when he

felt the pistol in his back. 'Who are you?' he said. 'What in hell you want?'

'What difference does it make?' Shawnee asked, pulling Manny's pistol from its holster and putting it in his own belt. 'You two started shooting at me without asking me jack shit. Seems you have a policy of shoot first, ask later.'

Cephus was silent.

'Enough talk, Cephus,' Shawnee growled. 'Into the house. Your sister will be here in a couple of minutes and we want to surprise her.'

Shawnee pushed Cephus toward the house and they entered through the back door. Shawnee pushed his captive down on a chair and said, 'We're going to play mouse. The first one who squeaks loses.' He cocked the Colt's hammer to emphasize his meaning.

They heard Beryl Cephus approach outside, leading Candy. She led the horse into the shed and tied it alongside the other two animals.

As she walked into the back door, she

was talking. 'Manny, have you seen anything of that sneaky bastard? I found his horse . . . '

Beryl was a heavy-set woman with rough features, bearing an unhappy resemblance to her brother except she looked even meaner. She stopped in her tracks and mid sentence when she saw Shawnee standing behind her brother holding a pistol to his head. 'What in hell is going on?' she demanded.

'Put the rifle down on the floor, Beryl,' Shawnee said. When she hesitated he added, 'Put it down now unless you want me to spray you with your brother's brains.'

With rage clouding her face Beryl Cephus placed her rifle on the floor.

'Now kick it over here,' Shawnee said.

Beryl shoved the rifle with her foot and it scooted almost to her brother's feet.

'Now, that we understand each other, I'm going to ask Manny here some questions; actually only one question. If

I get a reasonable answer, then I leave here on my horse and the two of you never see me again. Understood?'

Neither of them answered.

Shawnee pushed the Colt's barrel into Manny's right ear and shoved hard. 'God damn it!' he shouted. 'Do you understand?'

Manny held his head steady and mouthed, 'Yeah.' Beryl watched him and said, 'Yeah.'

'All I need to know is where is Marsh Kennebec?' Shawnee said.

'Go to hell!' Cephus spat.

Shawnee grabbed Cephus's left arm by the wrist, pulled the hand above its owner's head and shot the middle finger off.

Cephus screamed and Beryl's hands flew to her mouth. Cephus grabbed his left hand with his right and continued screaming.

As Cephus babbled, Shawnee repeated his question. 'Where is Marsh Kennebec?'

Cephus moaned but didn't answer.

Shawnee looked at Beryl and asked,

'Do you know where Marsh Kennebec went?'

She shook her head rapidly and murmured, 'No, I don't know. Please, let me tie up his hand.'

'No,' Shawnee said. 'I'm going to ask the question again, and if he doesn't answer, I'm going to start shooting off his toes. I've got five shots left. Think you can stand the pain, Manny? Oh look, Manny. Your finger is on the floor there. You want your toes to join it?'

'No, don't!' Manny pleaded. 'I'll tell you.'

Shawnee started to say, 'That's a smart boy,' but he didn't get all the words out. He was looking at Manny but from the corner of his eye, he saw Beryl make a quick move with her right hand. It disappeared behind her for a fraction of a second and when it reappeared, it held a nickel-plated pistol. As Shawnee ducked behind Cephus, she raised the pistol and fired. The shot was high.

Shawnee fired as Manny jumped out

of the chair and Shawnee's shot creased Beryl's left shoulder, making her cry out. Manny turned and thrust at Shawnee's face with his right hand and, with his mangled left, tried to hold Shawnee's shooting arm. Shawnee shook his arm free and clubbed at Manny's head with his pistol. Manny fell to the floor on his face on top of Beryl's rifle. Beryl was nowhere to be seen. Suddenly, Manny rolled over, bringing the rifle barrel up to get a shot. Shawnee fired virtually point blank into his chest. Manny dropped the rifle but he reached up and grabbed Shawnee's leg and pulled. Shawnee's left boot slid on Manny's blood and, as he went down, he spotted Beryl rushing at him with an axe held high above her head. Instinctively, Shawnee fired two shots into her chest. She collapsed, the axe falling from her hands. Her momentum carried her forward and she fell on top of Shawnee and her brother.

★ ★ ★

It was almost sundown when Shawnee returned to Juno driving Beryl's wagon with Candy and Manny's horse tied to the tailgate. In the wagon bed were two silent forms wrapped in sheets. Shawnee, his clothes splotched with dried blood, stepped down from the wagon and leaned against it as people drifted out of the café and the general store to look at the two bodies in the wagon.

The Ansleys and Henry Stein walked up and peered into the wagon.

Shawnee said, 'It's Manny Cephus and his sister Beryl. They started shooting at me before they even knew why I was there. When I finally caught both of them, all I wanted was for Manny to answer one question and I would have left them in peace. But they wouldn't have it the easy way.'

Shawnee drew some money from his pocket. 'Here's the money I found on Manny. It ought to be enough to bury both of them.' He looked at Ansley. 'You do have a cemetery here, don't you?'

'Oh yes,' Ansley said, taking the money. 'We'll take care of the burial.'

'Thanks very much,' Shawnee said. 'I'm plumb tuckered out and I've got to wash off my hands and knees and get 'em doctored. So if you folks will excuse me?'

Shawnee untied Candy and led her to the stable for a good night's sleep. He knew he needed the sleep if he could get it. He would have to go on the road tomorrow to find Alfred Tutt now that Manny Cephus wouldn't be doing any talking.

'Stupid son of a bitch!' he said under his breath. He had never understood the notion of honour among thieves.

6

It was a six-day trip to Fort Stockton taking the most direct route. Shawnee followed the Diablo north to Pecan Spring where he stocked up on water. From there he went directly west until he reached the Pecos River. He followed the Pecos to Camp Lancaster, then headed west or about seven points north of west to Fort Stockton. He felt the night creatures were bent on keeping him awake with their calls, yips, squawks and howls. It wasn't actually the night creatures; their regular sounds usually didn't bother him, so he suspected sleep was reluctant to come because he had killed a woman and he was afraid that the voices would come back. Never mind that his options at the time had been severely limited; he was on the floor tangled up with her brother's body and she had raised an axe on high to split him down the middle. Somewhere in that noisy brain of his there was perpetual confusion between what he observed with his own eyes and what his father had taught him about females being companions and objects of affection.

Shawnee spent his first night in Fort Stockton sleeping in a bed. He got Candy bedded down in the stable in back of the hotel, got a hot bath after bullying the staff into providing fresh hot water, then went to bed and slept for a solid nine hours. He woke the next morning with a raging appetite and a greatly improved disposition. He knew that, in wrestling with his mental conflicts on the trail, he had come out on top.

After breakfast, Shawnee visited the town marshal, Coler Baumgartner. The marshal was a big man, around forty years old, thick around the middle and with a florid complexion which hinted at an excessive fondness for alcohol.

Shawnee introduced himself and said he was looking for information. The marshal told him to fire away and he would help if he could.

Shawnee said, 'There's a man originally from these parts I need to find to get some information.'

'Who's that?' the marshal asked, seemingly in a helpful mood.

'Alfred Tutt,' Shawnee answered.

The marshal's face clouded and the pleasant smile departed. 'Why do you want Alfred Tutt?' Baumgartner demanded.

Here we go again, Shawnee thought. He said, 'As I said, I think he may know the whereabouts of someone I'm looking for. I tried to get the information from a friend of his a ways back, Manny Cephus, but it didn't go too well.'

'I've heard of him,' Baumgartner said, frowning. 'What happened?'

'I had to kill him. He was so scared of the law, he tried to shoot me before I even told him I wasn't a lawman.'

'Who you looking for?' the sheriff asked, his eyes narrowing.

'A murderer,' Shawnee answered. 'A man wanted for murdering a man and a woman back in Eagle Pass.'

'You going to tell me his name?' the marshal asked, his tone growing more hostile.

Shawnee sat and looked the marshal in his eyes for a long, silent moment. Then he said, 'Nope, I don't think so.'

As the marshal's face grew livid, Shawnee got to his feet, tipped his hat and said, 'I'll be going now. Thanks for your time.'

Shawnee was out the door on the boardwalk when the marshal grabbed his shoulder from behind.

'Just a damned minute, Lanigan!' the marshal shouted.

Shawnee twisted away from the man and took two steps back. 'Are you going to arrest me?' he barked. 'If you are, you better cook up a damned good story.'

Several passers-by stopped to take in the argument.

Baumgartner looked at Shawnee's

posture, the pistol on his hip and his defiant expression. He glanced around at the citizens staring in surprise.

'What's it going to be, Marshal?' Shawnee demanded.

'Not today,' the lawman muttered, turned and walked back into his office.

Shawnee looked at the bystanders, tipped his hat to a lady and walked up the street. With considerable effort, he held his temper and walked into the nearest saloon. He ordered a whiskey, downed it, ordered another, then turned to survey the room. And there she was, dimpling when she smiled, blonde, blue-eyed and squeezing up out of her bodice was the plumpest, creamiest, most mouth-watering pair of breasts he had seen in days and, to make matters worse, on one of them, he could see just the hint of pink peeking over the edge of the black material.

'I can almost see your puppy noses,' he said.

'I'm Happy,' she said, smiling wickedly.

'I'm glad,' Shawnee answered.

He knew he was done for and the rest of the day was lost to the investigator, claimed by the rouée.

★ ★ ★

Shawnee awoke to the sound of a door latch. Happy was asleep beside him, snoring a soft feminine snore. Without moving his head, Shawnee glanced around the room. An almost full moon was low in the sky and its light was coming through the two windows overlooking the street. The movement of a shadow caught his eye. The shadow stopped at the chair where he had hastily draped his pants before partaking of the varied delights offered by the aptly named Happy.

Shawnee almost snorted in disgust both at the thief and himself. 'Probably Happy's pimp,' he said to himself.

The shadowy thief, with his back to the bed, was busily extracting things from Shawnee's wallet. Shawnee pushed

87

himself up with one hand and pulled his feet under his body simultaneously. Without hesitation he leaped across the foot of the bed.

Shawnee grabbed the thief's shoulders and his knees dug into the man's back. The impact carried them to the floor; the thief's face hit the floor with a loud crack. Shawnee leapt to his feet, seized the thief by the collar and crotch, yanked him erect and jerked him to the open window. Too late, the thief realized his would-be victim's intentions; he screamed and clawed at the windowsill. He arced through the air, arms and legs flailing, until he hit the ground under the second-floor window.

Happy, shocked awake by the struggle and the scream, sat up in the bed wide-eyed. Shawnee lit the coal-oil lamp, replaced the chimney and looked at her with hard eyes.

'Was that your pimp?' he growled.

'What do you mean?' she asked in a panicked voice. 'Is Irv dead?'

She jumped out of the bed and

retrieved her dress from the floor, holding it in front of her body. She went to the window and peered out.

'He's moving, he's still alive,' she cried plaintively.

'I said, 'is he your pimp?' Lie to me and I'll beat you so hard, you won't be able to stand up for a month, much less screw and rob some dumb cowboy.'

Her lower lip pushed out and tears started down her cheeks.

'Please don't hurt me, Shawnee! He made me do it,' she wailed. 'He carries a knife and he said he'd cut me if I didn't do what he said.'

'Who is he and what did he tell you to do?'

She glanced out the window again.

'His name is Irv Gaskin,' she said, sobbing between words. 'He told me to unlock the door after you went to sleep and then stay in the bed with you.'

Then her words came out in a rush. 'Oh, he's so mean to me. I want to get away from him but he won't let me. He said he'd kill me if I tried to run away. I don't want to rob people but I can't help it.'

The scowl faded from Shawnee's face and he smiled cynically. 'What would you do if you got away, Happy? How would you make a living?'

'I'd go back home to Midlothian and ask my momma and daddy to take me back in,' she said.

'You sound almost convincing,' Shawnee said.

'I mean it,' she wailed, the tears coming again. 'Help me, Shawnee. Last night when we were making love, I could tell you liked me. I could be so good for you, Shawnee. I could be anything you asked. Help me please.'

'Look, lady,' Shawnee said in disgust, 'I'm on my way to do a job of work. I can't be screwin' around helping whores get away from their pimps.'

'But you shoot people for a living,' she sobbed. 'He wouldn't be hard to kill.'

Shawnee bristled. 'You got that wrong, girly, I ain't no cheap gunny,' he barked. 'I'm a problem solver. Now get your ass out of here!'

Shawnee bent over and picked up his wallet from the floor where Gaskin had dropped it. He gathered his money from the floor, grunted in satisfaction and shoved the wallet back in the right hip pocket of his jeans. He looked up at Happy who was standing in the middle of the room, looking hurt.

'You still here?' he growled.

Hurriedly and with a whimper, she pulled on her undergarments, gathered her clothes and disappeared out the door.

People were stirring in the street, attracted by Gaskin's plunge. Shawnee watched as a passer-by helped the pimp to his feet. Gaskin staggered away, wobbling on his feet and uncertain as to the direction he wanted to take. Shawnee got dressed as dawn lightened the eastern sky and strolled to the nearest café for breakfast. He had finished his meal when a man dressed in a grey suit and white shirt entered the café and stopped at Shawnee's table.

'I have something to discuss with you,' the man said. 'May I sit down?'

'Make yourself at home,' Shawnee said, gesturing at the chair opposite him. The man sat, leaned close and said, 'I'm John Milam. I'm with the local bank.'

Shawnee nodded and waited.

'I understand you are looking for Alfred Tutt.'

Shawnee said, 'You understand correctly. How did you come by that information?'

'I have a friend who overheard Sheriff Baumgartner talking to someone yesterday and he passed the information along to me. This morning, I was on my way to the bank to prepare for an early meeting with a local cattleman and I saw you come in here. I wanted to catch you before you got out of town, so I locked up the bank and here I am. I can tell you where Tutt is. But you better steer clear of Coler Baumgartner,' Milam said earnestly.

'You don't have to tell me twice to stay away from that gentleman,' Shawnee said.

Milam smiled grimly. 'Baumgartner is an old friend of Tutt's,' he whispered. 'The two of them grew up together, like two peas in a pod. I have reason to believe he will protect Tutt, by any means at his disposal.'

'I figured there was something like that going on,' Shawnee said, nodding. 'Tutt is a bad man. How come this town lets Baumgartner look out for him the way he does?'

'Most people don't know,' Milam answered. 'The ones who do know either don't care or they're scared of Coler.'

'Where is Tutt?' Shawnee asked.

'He's in Puta Gorda.'

'Fat whore?' Shawnee said, frowning. 'What kind of town is that?'

Milam chuckled. 'It's not on any map. It's no more than a few buildings off the road to Pecos, about ten miles from here. I understand he keeps company with a woman who has a shack there.' He reached into his inside coat pocket and removed a folded piece of paper. 'Before I left the bank, I made a sketch of the route to Puta Gorda. I thought you might find it useful. It shows some major checkpoints which may help you.'

'What's the woman's name?' Shawnee asked, examining the map.

'I don't know. Sorry.'

'I'll find him. There can't be too many places to hide in Puta Gorda,' Shawnee said. 'What's your interest in this, by the way?'

Milam glanced around to make certain no one was eavesdropping. 'I do not care for our sheriff. I think he's more criminal than lawman. Being in the banking business, I'm concerned with the prosperity of the town and the county. I don't think having a criminal pretending to enforce the law is good for business.'

Shawnee nodded his understanding and got to his feet. 'Mr Milam,' he said, extending his hand, 'I thank you very much for your help. If I'm successful, I'll let you know.'

'Good hunting,' Milam said.

The two men walked out the café on to the boardwalk and Milam turned his steps towards the bank in the next block. The livery stable was across the street half a block away. Shawnee was stepping off the boardwalk to cross the street when, from his left, a shot rang out. He felt splinters hit his face and he dived into the street, pulling his Colt. He hit the dirt on his stomach and rolled over quickly. Another shot kicked up dust where he had been. He rolled on to his back and pointed his weapon towards where the shots had been fired. A man stood on the boardwalk, his face a grotesque caricature, the eyes blackened and swollen almost shut, the nose a swollen protuberance. Irv Gaskin was looking for revenge.

7

Gaskin's next shot hit the dirt only inches from Lanigan's head.

'Drop it!' Shawnee held his pistol on Gaskin's chest and jumped to his feet. 'I don't want to kill you.' He was vaguely aware of people running for cover.

Gaskin squinted at Lanigan. 'Go to hell!' He fired again.

The shot was wide and Lanigan returned fire. The slug hit Gaskin in the middle of his chest, shattered his sternum, passed through his heart and lodged in his spine. He went down like a sack of grain.

Shawnee holstered his weapon and walked over to Gaskin. The dead man's left arm was in a sling. There were bandages on his neck and right arm. His face was swollen beyond recognition.

'You poor dumb bastard!' Shawnee said to the body, shaking his head. 'Why couldn't you leave well enough alone?'

The curious were starting to gather around the body. 'Who is that?' someone asked. 'That looks like Irv Gaskin's belt buckle,' another said. 'Who is Irv Gaskin?' someone else asked.

'He was one of our leading citizens,' a voice boomed, drowning out the others.

Shawnee looked up at the speaker. It was Baumgartner and he was pointing a single-action .45 directly at Shawnee's head.

'You're under arrest, drifter,' Baumgartner shouted. 'Take your pistol out of the holster with two fingers and drop it on the ground. If I see three fingers on it, I'll blow your damn brains out!'

With his thumb and forefinger, Shawnee lifted the pistol out of its holster and dropped it to the ground.

'Now the knife!' the sheriff ordered.

Shawnee carefully lifted the knife from its sheath and dropped it to the ground.

A deputy came running up and stopped beside the sheriff. He looked at Shawnee, then at the sheriff, wide-eyed.

'Pick up those weapons,' Baumgartner ordered.

The deputy did as he was told.

'What is going on here, Sheriff,' someone yelled. Shawnee glanced at the speaker. It was Milam.

Milam continued, 'Why are you arresting this man? That thug fired at him three times before he defended himself. It was self-defence. I saw the whole thing.'

'Shut the hell up, banker boy,' Baumgartner growled. 'You can tell it to the judge. As far as I'm concerned, I'm goin' to hold this drifter for murder until the judge gets here.'

There was a murmur from the bystanders. The sheriff told the deputy to keep his gun on Shawnee, then turned and addressed the collecting crowd.

'This man shot down one of our citizens in cold blood. He's going to be held for trial and anyone who tries to get in my way on this will go on trial with him.'

Baumgartner turned, surveying the faces around him. Some turned quickly and went about their business. Others turned to their companions and whispered. Only Milam would meet Baumgartner's eyes.

'Still looking out for your no-good friends, eh, Coler?' Milam asked.

'You keep your damn' mouth shut if you know what's good for you,' Baumgartner snarled.

The remaining spectators hurried away.

'Let's go,' Baumgartner said to Shawnee, gesturing down the street toward the jail with his pistol. 'Lead the way, Deputy.'

Shawnee followed the deputy and Baumgartner followed Shawnee at a safe distance. The three-man parade attracted attention on both sides of the street until they reached the jail. The deputy opened the door and held it as Shawnee and the sheriff walked in. The deputy then dumped Shawnee's pistol and knife on the sheriff's desk and hurried to open the door to the cells. He went through it, unlocked a cell door and then patted Shawnee's pockets. He removed his wallet and a pocket knife and added them to the items on the desk. The sheriff prodded Shawnee into the cell.

'There's just one more thing before I lock you up, Lanigan,' Baumgartner said.

Shawnee turned to face the sheriff just as the big man reached out and slammed him in the side of his head with his pistol. Shawnee reeled and fell to the stone floor. The sheriff grunted in satisfaction and slammed the cell door shut with a loud clang. The deputy looked at the sheriff in amazement.

Baumgartner looked at the deputy and said, 'What?'

The deputy shook his head and dropped his eyes, saying nothing.

The sheriff went out into his office and sat down behind his desk. He reached into the top drawer, pulled out a bottle of whiskey and poured a generous shot into his coffee mug.

'When's the judge coming around this time?' the deputy asked, attempting to sound casual.

''Bout three weeks,' the sheriff replied, looking pleased. 'We'll have a hearing to see whether or not to try this bird when he gets here. If it's like that scrawny bastard Milam said, it was self-defence, we'll turn him loose. By the way, run on down to the undertaker's place and see about a county burial for that pile of shit Gaskin. We can't leave 'im lying in the street like that.'

★   ★   ★

Shawnee came to his senses but didn't try to get up for a while to make certain that the sheriff wasn't still within arm's reach and that none of his bones was broken. Hearing nothing, he moved his limbs, then gingerly touched the side of his head with his fingers. He felt blood in his hair and on the side of his face.

His cheek-bone was sore as hell. He got to his feet and his head reeled. He grabbed one of the bars to steady himself. After a moment, he made his way to the cot. He sat on the filthy, straw-stuffed, canvas mattress and tried to evaluate his situation. However, the pain from the blow to his head and his anger made it impossible to think logically. He sat with his elbows on his knees and his head in his hands until he heard his name mentioned in the outer office. He got up, went to the bars and strained to hear what was being said.

The sheriff was arguing with someone who wanted to talk to Shawnee. Obviously, the sheriff wanted no one to talk to his new prisoner but the other voice belonged to someone who knew something about the law, or at least more than the sheriff. In a few moments the door to the office opened and a middle-aged man wearing a dark suit appeared. The sheriff followed.

The man turned and looked at the sheriff expectantly, waiting for the lawman to unlock the cell door.

'I'd like to talk to my client in confidence, Sheriff,' the man said. 'Could you let me into his cell?'

'If I do, I'll have to lock you in,' the sheriff growled.

'That's acceptable,' the man replied.

With ill-disguised impatience, the sheriff unlocked the cell door, held it while the attorney entered, then relocked it.

'I'll be back in a half-hour to let you out,' Baumgartner said.

'I'll call you when I have finished talking to my client, Sheriff,' the attorney replied coolly. 'I assume someone will be in the office when I call?'

The sheriff went out and slammed the door.

'I am amazed he doesn't drag his knuckles when he walks,' the attorney chuckled, winking at Shawnee. He held out his hand and said, 'I'm Lee J. Clark, attorney at law. Mr Milam down at the bank asked me to talk to you. By the way, what happened to your face?'

'The sheriff took out a little frustration on me before he locked me up,' Shawnee said. 'But I'm happy to see you. I plumb run out of ideas.'

Clark gestured at the cot, the only place to sit, and the two men sat down.

The attorney said in a low voice, 'Milam told me what you were about before that unfortunate Gaskin fellow tried to kill you. What was that all about, anyway?'

Shawnee filled in the attorney on the night's events.

'I never cease to be amazed,' Clark said, shaking his head. 'This is a primitive land we live in! But let's get down to brass tacks. I'm going to get you out of here by posting bond. Milam has agreed to put up the amount.'

'That's mighty white of Mr Milam,' Shawnee said, puzzled, 'but he hardly knows me. How come he's willing to put up money for me?'

Clark nodded and smiled. 'He knows you are trying to find Tutt to get information out of him. He dislikes both Tutt and Baumgartner and if you are lined up against both of them, he's for you. And time is of the essence. We need to get you on your way before Baumgartner has time to notify Tutt of your quest.'

Shawnee noticed that the pain in his head had decreased considerably. 'That sounds mighty good to me,' he said. 'How soon can you get me out of here?'

'As soon as we can get the magistrate sobered up enough to listen to us,' Clark said. 'Don't mention this to anyone. I don't want the sheriff to know about it until it's done.'

'You can count on me.' Shawnee said.

Later in the afternoon, after Shawnee had lunched on bread and bad coffee, he again heard loud voices in the office. He recognized one of them as Clark's. Suddenly the door to the office swung open and Clark walked through.

'I got you out of here, Shawnee,' he said. 'I suggest you waste no time in completing your task.'

A deputy unlocked the cell door and Shawnee picked up his hat and walked out. He went to the sheriff's desk and asked for his personal property. The sheriff glowered, opened the desk, and took out Shawnee's wallet, pocket knife, belt knife and pistol. Shawnee peered into his wallet and looked at the sheriff.

'Where's the money that was in this wallet?' he demanded.

The sheriff smiled and said, 'What money? That wallet was empty as an orphan's belly when you came in here.'

'You son of a bitch!' Shawnee snarled. 'You're not only a cowardly bastard, you're a damned thief!' He started for the sheriff.

Clark grabbed his arm and said in his ear, 'No, not now, Shawnee. We'll tend to that later.'

Baumgartner had reached for his pistol and had it halfway out of the holster when Clark stopped Shawnee.

'Get his ass outta my sight!' the sheriff roared.

Shawnee and Clark walked out the door onto the boardwalk. Milam awaited them.

'So he robbed you?' Milam asked.

'He damn sure did!' Shawnee answered.

'Here,' Milam said, handing Shawnee a roll of bills. 'It's just fifty dollars but I figure it will get you where you're going and back here in time for court in three weeks.'

When Shawnee looked surprised, Milam said, 'I figured he'd keep anything valuable he could get his hands on, and you were going to need some expense money. Now get going before Baumgartner has a chance to warn Tutt.'

Shawnee thanked the two men profusely and headed for the livery stable. He saddled Candy, got his rifle out of the stableman's lockup and paid him off. He rode by the café, picked up some food for the trail and set out for Puta Gorda.

It was late afternoon when Shawnee rode out of Fort Stockton with great relief. He pulled Milam's map out of his pocket and consulted it. He wanted to put as many miles between himself and that unpleasant place as he could and he urged Candy to a gentle lope. By the time the sun was setting he started to feel hunger pangs and rode off the west side of the road into a grove of mesquite trees. He gave the horse a drink from the canvas water bag he carried for that purpose. He poured the water into the crown of his hat and she drank till it was gone. He was gnawing on a fried chicken leg from his saddlebag when he heard the sound of hoofs.

It was a horse running hard through the gathering darkness. Shawnee mused: whoever the rider was, he was pushing his horse very hard to get to no place in particular. What little light still hung in the western sky was behind Shawnee but gave weak illumination to the horse and rider as they galloped by. The rider was peering straight ahead down the road as if expecting to see something or someone. As the rider rode past, Shawnee recognized the rider's hat and ugly profile. It was Coler Baumgartner!

Shawnee felt a thrill of satisfaction cascade down his spine. He had hoped Baumgartner might somehow try to interfere with him one more time. As far as Shawnee was concerned, Coler Baumgartner had forfeited his free pass to life, liberty and the pursuit of happiness.

Shawnee finished his solitary meal, walked Candy back to the road and remounted. Since he was not familiar with the road and was unwilling to take too many chances, he nudged Candy to a walk and evaluated his position. *When Baumgartner reaches Puta Gorda, it will take him only minutes to learn I haven't been there. He didn't see me on the road for one of two reasons: I had not yet left for Puta Gorda or I had gone somewhere else. He will find it easy to prepare for the first reason. He'll set up an ambush, perhaps with the help of his friend Tutt, and wait. If*

I do not appear in a reasonable amount of time, he will grow tired of waiting and assume the second reason.

By moonlight, Shawnee consulted Milam's crude map, looking for an arroyo spanned by a wooden bridge that lay about two miles south of Puta Gorda. The best way to defeat an ambush was not to ride into it. He would leave the road at the bridge, feel his way carefully to the west of the little settlement and approach from the north. That way he might be able to surprise the ambushers.

He kept Candy at a steady walk. He had all night to gain his objective and if he had to fight on someone else's home ground, he would rather fight in daylight.

The voices in his head were trying to get his attention when Candy's hoofs beat out a slow tempo on the wooden bridge. He reached the end of the short bridge and without pausing turned off the road to the left. By the moonlight he made out the edge of the arroyo and followed it on cautiously, making certain he did not come upon an unseen wash and possibly break one of the horse's legs. He came to a dry gully, one of the arroyo's feeders pointing to the north. He turned and followed it until it faded into a series of smaller gullies. Up ahead to his right, he saw a flicker of light, perhaps a coal-oil lantern showing through a hut's window. He pressed on and soon saw a few more points of light, clustered together in the darkness. 'Puta Gorda,' he whispered to the darkness.

He rode on until the lights were behind him and to his right, then turned to the east. He continued until he came upon the road going north out of the settlement. Just as dawn was showing in the east, he turned south on the road. Shawnee felt weariness all the way to his bones. As he reached the first shacks on the outskirts of the settlement, the sun was up. He saw movement down the road, on the other side of the settlement. There was a man pacing beside the road. Watching carefully in the gaining light, he saw a man on the other side of the road sitting on something, perhaps a wooden box. That man was gazing south down the road, waiting.

It was Baumgartner.

8

For a split second, Shawnee thought about kicking Candy into a gallop and charging the two men with rifle and pistol blazing. But experience stifled the impulse. Firing from a galloping horse is an odds-against proposition. Not only does the rider's accuracy go to hell, the easier target for a man defending himself from a man on horseback is the horse. Bring down the horse and the rider will get a shoulder or a leg broken all to hell or, if the shooter is lucky, his neck. Shawnee couldn't even consider the notion of sacrificing Candy for an ill-considered shoot-out that would probably end badly.

Shawnee pulled Candy to the side of the road and found a hitching post at the side of a building. He dismounted, patted her neck, chambered a round in the rifle and replaced it in the magazine, put a sixth round into the cylinder of his Colt and started sauntering casually alongside the few buildings on his side of the road. He turned to the right between two buildings and gained the alleyway behind them. He strolled along unhurriedly to avoid attracting attention. Eventually he could go no further behind the row of Puta Gorda's run-down buildings. He walked alongside the last building and into the street. The man Shawnee assumed to be Tutt saw him first but the sight of another cowboy strolling by meant nothing to him. Then Baumgartner saw him.

'Good God a'mighty!' Baumgartner yelled, reaching for his pistol. Shawnee raised the rifle, sighted along the open sight and fired. Baumgartner spun to his left as if kicked by a horse. Shawnee levered another round into the Winchester's chamber.

Baumgartner held on to his pistol and turned back toward Shawnee immediately. He fired but the distance was too great for handgun accuracy and the slug sizzled past Shawnee like an angry hornet. Shawnee raised the rifle, sighted along the barrel without using the sights and fired again. The sheriff lurched backwards, his mouth opened but no sound came out. His knees folded and he fell to the ground.

Tutt got his wits about him at last and fired a quick shot with his pistol. The shot went wide and Shawnee yelled, 'Drop it or I'll kill you!' Tutt looked at Shawnee sighting him along the barrel of a rifle and hesitated.

'Drop it or die!' Shawnee yelled.

Tutt dropped the pistol and raised his hands.

Shawnee smiled grimly. At last he had someone still living who could tell him about Marsh Kennebec.

Ignoring the curious few emerging from the buildings of Puta Gorda, Shawnee made certain that Alfred Tutt carried no other weapons, picked up his prisoner's pistol and told him to put his arms down.

'Let's see what's left of Sheriff

115

Baumgartner,' Shawnee said without emotion.

With Tutt moving his legs stiffly in front, they walked across the street to where the body lay sprawled.

'Take out his wallet,' Shawnee instructed.

Tutt bent over and pulled the dead man's wallet out of his hip pocket.

'Take one hundred and sixty dollars out of it and hand it to me.'

Tutt counted out one hundred sixty dollars, handed it to Shawnee, and stood waiting for instructions.

'Put the rest in your own pocket and let's go,' Shawnee said.

'Where to?' Tutt asked in a shaky voice, stuffing the money into a pocket.

'Your place,' Shawnee answered matter-of-factly.

Tutt turned and walked up the street. Shawnee followed by two paces and held his .44 on the small of his prisoner's back. When they reached a shack and Tutt said, 'Here we are,' Shawnee holstered his weapon.

Tutt's woman, a small, dark, ugly

woman with unkempt black hair, met them at the door. She stepped aside as the two men walked in and asked Tutt something in Spanish.

Tutt answered her in Spanish. Shawnee knew enough of it to know that Tutt was telling her Baumgartner was dead.

The woman looked at Shawnee with a wild stare, muttered something that sounded like a snarl and ran to where she had been cooking and grabbed a knife.

Tutt cried out, 'No, no, Dolores!'

The woman held the knife at waist level and started toward Shawnee. Shawnee drew quickly and put the pistol to the back of Tutt's head.

'Put it down or I kill him,' Shawnee commanded. 'Then I'll kill you.'

When Dolores gave no indication that she understood Shawnee's words, Tutt screamed, 'God damn it, Dolores!' Then, in Spanish he yelled, 'Put the knife down now or he's goin' to scatter my brains.'

The woman's hand dropped to her

side, somewhat reluctantly Shawnee thought. She turned and walked back to the kitchen table and put the knife down.

'All right, Alfred,' Shawnee said, holstering his pistol, 'have your wife put some coffee on and let's talk.'

'She ain't my wife,' Tutt replied. 'You think I'd marry a woman that damned ugly?'

When Shawnee looked surprised, Tutt added, 'But she's one hell of a cook.'

As it happened, the woman called Dolores had already made coffee and now poured two cups for Shawnee and Tutt. The men sat at the crude table in what served as the kitchen of the two-room shack.

Shawnee sipped his coffee, made a wry face and said, 'Tutt, I know you were with Marsh Kennebec in Eagle Pass when he killed Ward and Betsy Kincaid.'

'Oh, God,' Tutt whined. 'I knew that was goin' to be trouble. I din't have nothing to do with killing those folks. We din't even know what he was goin' to do when he wanted to stop at that house. You got to believe me.'

'I know you didn't pull the trigger on that couple; I talked to a witness,' Shawnee assured Tutt. 'Marsh Kennebec killed 'em and I'm going to take him back to Eagle Pass for trial or kill him. Now if I can't find out where Kennebec is holed up, I'm going to take you back instead. After all, the law considers you an accomplice and they'd just as soon stretch your neck as Kennebec's.'

Tutt's face sagged.

'But I'm not being paid for bringing you back,' Shawnee explained. 'I'm being paid for Kennebec, so I'd rather not fool with you.'

The sag became a relieved smile. Tutt asked, 'What do you want to know?'

'Where is Kennebec?' Shawnee asked.

'He's in La Perdida,' Tutt said. 'But don't tell him how you found out. He'd kill me, fer sure.'

'Where is La Perdida?' Shawnee

asked, frowning.

'It's on the Rio Grande, 'bout sixty or seventy mile up river from Presidio,' Tutt replied.

'I didn't think there was anything that far up from Presidio. You sure?'

'That's what Kennebec told us. He said that at one time La Perdida was on the Texas side of the river, then a big flood come and it ended up on the Mexican side. Nobody knows who it belongs to and there ain't no law there. It's a hideout. When the law comes lookin' for somebody, they just run over into Mexico where the law can't follow. They's some Mexican *bandidos* stay there for the same reason. They can hightail it to Texas if the *Federales* show up.'

'Something tells me they don't bother with schools and churches there,' Shawnee chuckled.

'Reckon not,' Tutt replied. 'By the way, I wanted to ask you, is Manny Cephus really dead?'

''Fraid so,' Shawnee replied. 'What

did Baumgartner tell you?'

Tutt seemed to gather his nerve, then he said, 'That you cut off Manny's fingers and toes one at a time trying to get him to tell you where Marsh Kennebec was and he wouldn't tell and you finally shoved a scattergun up his ass and blew his guts out.'

'I'll say one thing for that son of a bitch of a sheriff, he had one hell of an imagination,' Shawnee said in wonder. 'Actually, I never got a chance to ask Manny a damned thing. When I got to his place, he and his sister started shooting at me without even a howdy-do. I ended up killing both of them. If he had just talked to me, he'd still be alive and I never would have showed up here.'

'Damn!' Tutt exclaimed. 'Baumgartner had me so scared of you, I 'bout shit my drawers.'

'How else was he going to get you to set up an ambush for me?' Shawnee said, getting to his feet.

'You leavin'?' Tutt asked, surprised.

'Yep. You told me what I want to know so I'm going on about my business.'

'You goin' to tell the law 'bout me?'

'Nope,' Shawnee replied. 'Not unless I get pressed by 'em. My business is to get Kennebec. What you and the law do is just between you and the law. Far as I'm concerned, I'll never hear your name again.'

'I 'preciates that, Mr Lanigan,' Tutt said with a thin smile on his face.

'I ask only one thing in return, Tutt,' Shawnee said, pausing in the doorway.

'What's that?'

'That if the law comes looking for Baumgartner, you don't have any idea who it was he shot it out with,' Shawnee grinned.

'Fair enough!' Tutt replied and opened the door for his guest.

Shawnee walked back to where he had left Candy, led her to a watering trough, and fed her some oats. After she had had her oats, he mounted up and headed south at a trot. As he passed the place where the sheriff had fallen, Shawnee saw the body was still there but Baumgartner's horse, his pistol, his vest, his gun belt and his boots were gone. One of his big toes was showing through a hole in the sock. Someone had even taken his badge.

Shawnee leaned over and whispered in Candy's ear, 'They'd have taken his socks too if they hadn't been worn out. Whoever named this place knew what he was talking about.'

★ ★ ★

Shawnee made a leisurely trip back to Fort Stockton, sometimes dozing in the saddle. It was late afternoon when he arrived and he went straight to the bank. He tied up Candy in front and went in. Milam saw Shawnee come in and waved at him, then pointed to his office.

Shawnee sat down in a guest chair while Milam sat behind his mahogany desk.

'I just wanted to return this to you,' Shawnee said, handing the banker fifty dollars. In response to Milam's surprise, he explained, 'I had the opportunity to recover the funds taken from me illegally so I won't be needing your gracious loan. But I thank you very much, sir.'

Milam looked at the money in his hand and asked, 'Do I want to know how you recovered your funds?'

'No, sir, you do not.' Shawnee smiled.

'Then we'll leave it at that,' Milam said, looking satisfied. 'Did you get the information you were seeking?'

'I did, sir. And tomorrow morning, I strike out to complete the job I was commissioned to do. And by the way, I don't think the sheriff will be around to take me before the judge when he arrives. However, I plan on being here so you can recover your bond money.'

'Are you saying we will need a new sheriff here in Pecos County?' Milam asked.

'I think you probably will,' Shawnee

said. 'I hear tell he ran into a bit of trouble up in Puta Gorda. Of course, that could be just a rumour.'

Shawnee got to his feet and shook Milam's hand. 'Many thanks for helping me out like you did, Mr Milam. I'm beholden to you.'

'Nonsense,' Milam exclaimed. 'If you took care of our Baumgartner problem, you have already repaid your debt many times over. Goodbye and good luck.'

The next morning Shawnee visited the county surveyor, who had a large map of Texas. Together, he and the surveyor calculated that to reach La Perdida, if it did indeed lie on the Rio Grande seventy miles upriver from Presidio, a straight course to it from Fort Stockton would be west-southwest. But the surveyor recommended to Shawnee a route requiring crossing a minimum of mountains *en route* to the mysterious La Perdida.

He would go to Fort Davis, then south past the Bishop's Mitre to the north fork of the Alamito River. The

Alamito would take him to the Rio Grande about seven miles southeast of Presidio. From there he would go upriver to La Perdida. It would be a long journey over unforgiving terrain. Shawnee thought it prudent to invest in a pack animal and purchased a *burro* from the livery stable. The *burro* would carry the supplies, the small tent and other hardware, saving Candy for carrying only himself.

He stopped at the telegraph office and sent a message to Brick Kincaid saying that he was on his way to Presidio and that he had been charged with a crime in Fort Stockton which might delay his return.

As he rode out of Fort Stockton to the southwest, he told his horse, 'Candy, I have no idea of what's out there ahead of us. This may be the one that kills me.'

9

The Big Bend country was so called because the Rio Grande took a steady course to the southeast until it reached the border between the Mexican states of Chihuahua and Coahuila, then abruptly turned to the north-north-east until joined by the San Francisco. Thence it meandered back to a southeast course. The large triangle thus bordered on two sides by the river was called the Big Bend. When Shawnee left Fort Stockton and headed southwest, he was going into that country. The next leg of his trip took him to Fort Davis. He reprovisioned there and headed south.

Following the Alamito to the Rio Grande would be about a sixty-mile trip but he would be assured of a water supply for Candy and the donkey, Escamillo. Also, its banks found their way through the mountains and following them took most of the pain from traversing the mountainous and rugged countryside. Shawnee estimated he could make twelve miles a day in that terrain with the two animals.

He was nearing the end of his second day on the trail before he saw another person. He saw them at a distance, two men on horseback making their way northward on the same side of the river. They hailed him at some distance, then rode toward him, faces wreathed in smiles.

'Howdy,' the first one said as they drew near. 'Didn't expect to see anyone else out here (he pronounced it ou'chere) and it's a treat to run into someone. My name's Oscar Snell and this here's my riding partner, Doug Strang.'

Shawnee looked them over quickly. Strang had grey eyes that didn't seem to focus properly. Snell smiled all the time. Shawnee didn't like people who smiled all the time. He figured they were up to something. The men were filthy and their equipment was well used. They both carried stuffed gunny sacks across the backs of their saddles.

'Howdy,' Shawnee said. 'My name's John Jones.'

'Where you headin', Jones,' Snell asked.

'I'm on my way to Presidio,' Shawnee answered. 'I got an uncle there I'm going to pitch in with. Where you fellows heading?'

'We're on our way to Alpine,' Strang answered. 'Figured we'd follow the Alamito then go on up to Fort Davis. We got some business to take care of there.'

'Got any baccy?' Snell asked.

'Nope, don't use it. Sorry.'

'Well shucks,' Snell said. 'Hopin' I could buy some off you. But you're the smart one, if you don't use them coffin nails.'

'Never acquired the habit,' Shawnee said. 'Reckon it's saved me a peck of money over the years.'

Snell cackled. 'You probably right on that, mister. But how's things on up the way from where you come?'

'Not much going on,' Shawnee answered. 'Ain't seen no people, saw a couple of coyotes, plenty a'jack rabbits and a mess of lizards. Other than that, it's been a quiet trip.'

Shawnee glimpsed Strang eyeing Candy and the donkey. He did not like the look in the man's eyes, not because of the out-of-focus look, but for the covetousness with which he stared.

Shawnee asked, 'Any surprises the way you came? Anything I oughta be on the lookout for?'

'Nope, not a thing we saw. Heck, they's hardly anybody out here and if'n they're here, they ain't got nothin' so the highwaymen don't bother.' He cackled loudly.

'That's good to know,' Shawnee answered.

Snell said, 'Well, I reckon we'll be movin' on, try to make a few more miles afore sundown.'

130

'Good luck to you,' Shawnee said. 'I hope you have a safe trip.'

'Pleased to make your acquaintance, Mr Jones,' Strang said, his strange eyes gleaming.

'Same here,' Shawnee replied.

The two groups continued in their original directions.

When the sun was a hand's width above the horizon, Shawnee reined Candy to a halt at a level place high enough to be safe from rising water. The chances were small the river would fill but it was still spring and anything could happen. He unsaddled the horse and unloaded the donkey and led the animals down to the river. After tending to the animals, he pitched his tent facing north and built a small fire in front of it. He made coffee and heated a can of beans over the fire. He ate slowly, taking in the sounds and sights of the wild country settling down for the night. One time when he thought he heard a horse whinnying he glanced at Candy. Her ears were standing up. He

131

stared for a long time to the north, the direction from where the sound seemed to come. He stretched his arms and yawned, then made ready for sleep. He made sure the animals were tethered properly some thirty feet away, pitched his bedroll into the tent and crawled in after it.

The fire had burned down to glowing coals when he opened the tent's back flap, crawled out, taking his bedroll and his rifle, and made his way to where the animals were tethered. He spread the bedroll between Candy's front and rear hoofs and climbed into it.

Hardly an hour had passed when Candy moved her hoofs nervously and woke Shawnee. He lay still and listened, halting his own breathing. Then he heard it. The measured crunch of a two-legged beast walking on rocky, dry soil. Then there was another, overlapping the first.

Shawnee eased out of the sleeping bag and crawled away from the animals. He cradled the Winchester in the crook of his arm and waited. He thought if they thought they were going to Indian up on him, they needed a hell of a lot more experience than what they were showing. Then he saw the men by starlight, walking carefully toward his camp, both carrying pistols. The taller of the two, Strang, was in front. He made his way around the coals of the fire and extended his arm toward the open end of the tent. He fired four times, the flashes of the powder illuminating his face. Shawnee almost shuddered at the grinning pleasure on that face.

Strang bent down to look into the tent and suddenly straightened.

'He ain't in thar!' he exclaimed shrilly.

Shawnee levered a round into the rifle's chamber and both men swivelled toward him.

Shawnee fired and Strang pitched backwards with a loud cry. Snell raised his pistol and not having a visible target, fired wildly in Shawnee's direction, then turned and started running.

Shawnee ran after him.

It was rough going running over the rocky terrain but Shawnee stayed near enough to Snell to hear his running steps and the occasional stumble. Snell stopped three times and fired back at Shawnee. The shots were wide each time. As Snell ran through the darkness, Shawnee could hear the man gasping for breath.

Suddenly the sounds up ahead stopped. Shawnee stopped and listened. There were no running steps. He waited, listening and peering into the darkness. Snell was waiting, perhaps behind a low bush, waiting for Shawnee to make himself visible in the starlight. Shawnee bent down and felt around for a stone. He found one and pitched it in the direction Snell had gone. When it fell, it clicked and rattled against other rocks and a shot rang out. Shawnee saw the muzzle flash. He fired at the flash and was rewarded by a scream and the sound of more running.

Shawnee renewed his pursuit. He saw

Snell struggling up a hill, silhouetted against the sky.

'Stop, Snell!' he called.

Snell turned and pulled the trigger. Shawnee heard the metallic click of the hammer falling on expended cartridges and stepped forward carefully. Snell stood motionless, his pistol hanging loosely from his hand.

'Tell me one reason why I shouldn't kill you,' Shawnee said.

Snell gasped out in hope, 'I got stuff we took from some pilgrims a ways back. It's good stuff, I can share it with you . . . hell, I can give it all to you. You don't have to kill me.'

'Don't I?' Shawnee asked and fired the rifle point blank into Snell's chest.

★ ★ ★

The next morning, Shawnee found the men's horses where their riders had tied them before sneaking into his camp. He didn't want to be weighed down by extra livestock so he removed the saddles and bridles and turned the horses loose. There was no way to bury the bodies in the rocky soil without tools, so he left the brigands' bodies where they had fallen. He piled their goods, their gear as well as the spoils they had taken from those unfortunate 'pilgrims' beside the trail. It wasn't the first time he had 'made coyote meat' and he did it without emotion.

The next day, he found what was left of the 'pilgrims'. It appeared to have been a family. There was a wagon, a dead mule, clothing and household goods scattered about. The buzzards were enjoying a festive occasion among the bodies. Shawnee picked up a Bible with generations of names and birth dates inscribed in it. He studied the names and wished he had killed Strang and Snell more slowly.

In two more days, Shawnee reached the Rio Grande and turned right, following the water upstream to Presidio. There, he found a stable and left his two animals comfortable in stalls with fresh hay and oats and went in search of a bath, taking a change of clothes with him. He found a barbershop where he could get a hot bath for one dollar.

As he luxuriated in the bath, he asked the barber where was a good place to eat. The barber told him the cantina across the street was the best place in town to eat. After he had rid himself of trail dirt, sweat and whiskers, he strolled across the street to enjoy a sit-down meal.

The meal was greasy and highly spiced but was more than adequate. For Shawnee, after eating jerky and dipping beans out of air-tights, it was akin to dining at Delmonico's. Of course, he had never dined at Delmonico's but he had heard it was elegant. He sipped the last of his beer and looked around the room. A few Anglos sat around the dining room but most of the customers were Latinos. As each one finished his meal, he leaned back and lit a cigarillo or a roll-your-own and partook of it lustily, smiling in satisfaction as the smoke curled around his head. Shawnee watched, wondering what it would be like to enjoy such a thing.

As Shawnee reflected upon the pleasures of tobacco, an Anglo walked up to his table.

'I wanted to chat with you for a moment,' the stranger said. 'Mind if I sit down?'

'Help yourself. I reckon it's safe since nobody around here knows me so you can't damage your reputation.'

The stranger laughed, pulled back a chair and sat down. 'I'm Jack Burkard,' he said, extending his hand.

'Howdy,' Shawnee said, shaking the hand. 'I'm Shawnee Lanigan. What can I do for you?'

'Going to be in Presidio long, Mr Lanigan?' Burkard asked.

'Not if I can help it,' Shawnee replied. 'I'm just traveling through. I got some business to take care of up river.'

'Oh, what business you in?'

'I guess you could call it trouble-shooting,' Shawnee said after brief reflection. 'I just kind of solve problems for folks when the problem is not the concern of the law. I just give a helping hand, you might say.'

'Well, that's mighty interesting, Lanigan,' Burkard said with uncertainty. 'Is business good?'

'It has its ups and downs,' Shawnee answered, smiling.

'What I really wanted to ask you was if you'd like to get into a poker game. Me and some friends are gettin' together this evening down at Chucho's Cantina.'

'We talking about high-stakes poker here, Burkard?' Shawnee asked with a note of scepticism.

'No, not at all, just a friendly get-together,' Burkard answered.

'Well, I get up for that. 'Course, I can't afford to be losing my expense money so I'll have to play kind of close to the vest.'

'I understand perfectly, Lanigan.

Shoot, ain't none of us millionaires,' Burkard said, chuckling. 'Tonight then, 'bout seven o'clock at Chucho's.'

'I'll see you there,' Shawnee said.

Shawnee got one of the dozen rooms at the local hotel, stowed his gear, and took a nap. He awoke just shy of seven o'clock, pulled on his boots and strolled down to Chucho's.

There were five of them in the game: Burkard, his friends Jones and Brown, a wholesale dry goods salesman named Albright, who tended toward plumpness and baldness, and Shawnee. They had a room of their own just off the main room of Chucho's cantina. A strikingly attractive dark-eyed girl called Encarnacion served them tequila with salt and lemon. The girl wore a thin white cotton blouse cut low in front to show her remarkably firm breasts to best advantage. Also, Shawnee could not help but notice what he called her 'puppy noses' pressed against the flimsy material as a reminder of her femininity, as if anyone could overlook it.

140

The game went well and Shawnee won a few hands. He picked up immediately on Albright's tell, a bad hand brought a doleful look to his face, a good hand a smug grin. Burkard remained relaxed when he had a bad hand but he revealed a good hand by drumming two fingers of his left hand on the table as if impatient to finish the hand and claim his pot. Shawnee couldn't read Jones and Brown. In fact, both of them seemed bored with the whole process. Each time Encarnacion brought a round of drinks to the card players, she touched Shawnee on the arm or cheek in response to his admiring glances and murmurs of friendly affection. After an hour, she stood by his chair, her hand touching his shoulder or her leg brushing briefly against his hip. Shawnee became more and more distracted by her presence as the evening wore on and he grew careless about the number of tequilas he was drinking. He was operating in a tequila-induced haze when his luck suddenly turned bad. He became dimly aware of Burkard's tell disappearing when he or Albright were betting heavily. His last memory of the evening was standing up at the table and denouncing the host and his friend as highwaymen. There was a confused blur of voices and sounds, then unconsciousness.

10

Shawnee awoke lying on a hard surface in a dark, dank place. He slowly regained his vision and looked toward the single source of light in the room. When he saw vertical iron bars in the window, he knew he was in a jail cell. Then he realized his head hurt terribly and his mouth felt as though he had been lapping mud out of the Rio Grande. The voice of the old shaman was pronouncing doom in the Algonquin language and his mother was weeping.

Oh God! I've done it again, he told himself. His tongue seemed to have sprouted fur and the pain in his head seemed to worsen when he moved, so he lay still. He was still lying motionless when he heard the door to the outer office open. He opened his eyes and peered at the sound. A square-built

Latino wearing a marshal's badge stood outside the bars regarding him with slight amusement.

'*Buenas dias, amigo,*' the marshal said. 'Are you once more among the living?' he asked in a slight accent.

'Hell, I'm not sure just yet. Do dead men have headaches?' Shawnee answered.

'I never heard one complain,' the marshal answered, grinning.

'Then I must be alive,' Shawnee concluded.

'In either case, you might like some coffee. It is strong enough to make the dead walk.'

Shawnee got up and took the tin cup of coffee between the bars. He sipped at it cautiously, grimaced and took another sip.

'This coffee packs double,' he said.

'It should, we grind the Arbuckle's right here,' the marshal said. 'By the way, my name is Porfirio Gutierrez. I'm the town marshal.'

'I must have raised hell last night,' Shawnee mumbled, sipping at the coffee.

'*Sí!*' Gutierrez chuckled. 'You were going to war against all of the town.'

'I seem to remember being suckered into a set-up, a rigged poker game,' Shawnee said, frowning at the vague memory.

'By the time I arrived, the others had departed. Who were they?' Gutierrez asked.

'The ramrod was a fellow named Burkard,' Shawnee said. 'Then there was Jones and Brown.'

Gutierrez threw back his head and laughed. 'Those three *bandidos* have been doing the same thing with travelers for a long time.' He held his hands with curved fingers in front of his chest. 'And a beautiful *chiquita* was part of it and she had *los globos y las chupas*[1] to drive you wild. No?'

'True.'

'And she stood by your chair and rubbed you as if she could not wait for you to get your hot, sweaty hands on her.'

---

[1] Breasts and nipples

'True,' Shawnee said sadly, nodding, and feeling for his wallet. He pulled it out and opened it.

'Empty,' he said without surprise. 'I'm having the damndest time trying to hold on to my money.'

'You don't have to worry no more,' the marshal said. 'It's gone this time.'

'Looks like I'm going to have to find a grubstake to get out of town,' Shawnee muttered in disgust. 'You going to let me out of here?'

'Maybe,' Gutierrez said, shrugging his shoulders. 'Come on into the office and we'll talk.'

He produced a bunch of keys and unlocked the cell door. Shawnee retrieved his hat and followed the marshal into his office, still sipping the Arbuckle.

Gutierrez said, 'Sit down and tell me what you are up to in our town. Then maybe I let you go.'

'Keep it between me and you?' Shawnee asked.

'Why?' Gutierrez asked.

'Because if 'what I'm up to' gets to

the wrong people, I'm a dead man.'

Gutierrez frowned then raised his right hand as if taking an oath. 'Done!' he said.

Shawnee then explained the murder of his client's daughter and her husband, the name of the murderer, the contract he had taken on and his destination.

Gutierrez sat stunned for a moment, then crossed himself and said, '*Ay, mio Dios!* They will roast you like a hog on a spit in La Perdida.'

'Could be,' Shawnee agreed. 'You see why it's important no one knows about what I'm doing.'

The marshal was silent, looking at the floor and shaking his head. Then he looked up and spoke.

'We may be able to help one another,' he said cautiously. 'I need some help pretty soon here. I have only one deputy and the sheriff is at the other end of this damned big county. I have the funds to pay a month's salary for a deputy marshal. I will pay you that money for a couple of days' work if you agree to help me. Then you can go on your way to certain death in La Perdida.'

Shawnee cocked his head sideways and looked at Gutierrez with one eye. 'What would I be doing for you?' he asked suspiciously.

The marshal leaned forward in his chair and spoke in a low voice. 'I have had word there is a very bad man and his gang coming into town tomorrow. His name is Finn Slatter and he is very dangerous. He has been here before and he and his men drink and shoot their pistols and fool around with the *putas*,[1] get into fights with the locals and every once in a while they kill someone. There are too many of them for one little marshal and his deputy to take on.'

Shawnee leaned back and thought about it for a few seconds. 'How much money we talking about here?'

---

[1] Whores

'Forty dollars,' Gutierrez answered. 'It is not much, but you will die at La Perdida anyway so you won't be needing more.'

'How many of them are there?'

'Last time it was five. I don't know how many this time. The person who told me they were coming is an old friend. He overheard Slatter talking in *una rameria*[1] downriver and only heard their destination.'

Shawnee said, 'Well, I can't travel on thin air. I reckon I'll take that job.'

Gutierrez was almost ecstatic. He jumped up and produced a badge from his desk. 'Raise your right hand,' he said.

★ ★ ★

Finn Slatter and his four men rode into Presidio at sundown the day after Shawnee took his oath as a deputy marshal. Marshal Gutierrez had stayed

---

[1] Crude whorehouse

149

on the boardwalk in front of the city jail nearly all day, either sitting in a chair tilted back against the wall or standing and chatting with passing locals, most of whom he knew personally. He dispatched his only regular deputy, Hernando Cruz, to show Shawnee around town, hiding-places, haunts of the dangerous and vantage points from which to ambush the 'bad people', as he put it.

Slatter and his men left their horses at the livery stable and swaggered up the main street of town. They were loud, profane and intimidating as they barged their way along the boardwalk to Chucho's Cantina. Women and small children darted away as they approached and soon the street was almost devoid of people. Word spread quickly and decent folk went home and stayed behind locked doors.

Chucho was disgruntled when the gang clattered through the front door into his place. They would drink and eat and drink some more but didn't like to pay. Chucho had learned the hard way about dealing with Finn Slatter, especially when money was the subject. Moreover, his other customers fled when the gang walked in. No one would take the chance of angering Slatter or one of his gun-wearing men.

Cruz and Shawnee, seeing Slatter arrive in town, made their way back to the jail. They sat while Gutierrez briefed them on his plan. While he and Cruz visited Chucho's to speak to Slatter in a cordial manner and feel him out as to his intentions, Shawnee would enter the cantina by the back door, stay out of sight and listen to the conversation, or if necessary provide help if Slatter did not take kindly to their visit. Then after he and Cruz took their leave, Shawnee would go out the back door and re-enter Chucho's through the front door and pretend to be a customer. He would keep an eye on the gang until they tired or left the cantina.

'Do you think you can handle that?' Gutierrez asked.

'Sure,' Shawnee said. 'These birds don't know me. It might work out real good.'

'That's settled,' Gutierrez said. 'Let's go. Lanigan, take off your badge and put it in your pocket. We'll give you time to get in position, then Cruz and I will go in.'

Shawnee left the jail and walked across the street and down the boardwalk until he neared the cantina. He cut between two buildings and walked down the alley to Chucho's. He stopped at the back door, eased it open and peered in. There was no lantern in the short hall to the back door and he slipped through and into the darkness.

He eavesdropped on the banter among Slatter's men until one of them called out, 'Well looky here! It's my favourite town marshal. How you doin', Porfirio?'

'*Buenas noches*, Señor Slatter,' Gutierrez replied. 'We have not been honored by your presence in some months. We despaired, thinking perhaps bad luck had befallen you.'

Slatter laughed heartily. 'Sorry to disappoint you, Marshal. I'm still alive and kicking.'

'So I see,' the marshal replied. 'How long will you and your associates honour us with your presence?'

Shawnee peered around the corner so he could see Gutierrez. The marshal had pulled a chair out from a table and put a foot on it, leaning his elbows on his knee in a casual attitude. Cruz had positioned himself just inside the doorway; he could see the whole room.

Slatter answered, 'I ain't real sure. We are on our way upriver to do some visiting. We just stopped over here to wash the trail dust out of our gizzards with some of this coffin varnish old Chucho sells.'

'Upriver?' Gutierrez asked. 'There is nothing upriver from here until you get to El Paso. You are going to visit the lizards and the buzzards perhaps?'

Slatter laughed again. 'That's what I like about you, Porfirio, you got a sens'a humour.'

'In my work, it is necessary,' Gutierrez said. 'Life goes by too fast not to laugh now and again.'

Gutierrez cut his eyes at the door from where Shawnee was watching. It was very quick and subtle but Shawnee knew something was happening. Then he heard the steps. One of Slatter's men had gotten up from his table out of Shawnee's sight and was walking toward his hiding-place.

'Damn', Shawnee thought to himself, 'how could I forget somebody would have to piss?'

The man rounded the corner, saw Shawnee out of the corner of his eye, went into a half-crouch and reached for his pistol!

11

Shawnee threw his left hand into the air
and his right hand to his mouth, the
index finger to his lips. The gunman
stopped with his pistol halfway out of
its holster and looked at Shawnee
quizzically. Shawnee mouthed the word
'marshal' and pointed into the room
from where the man had come. The gunman released his weapon and Shawnee
took him by the arm and pointed at the
back door. They went through the door
to the outside and stopped on the path
to the outhouse.

'Who the hell are you, you dumb
bastard?' the gunman asked angrily. 'I
could've shot your ass.'

Shawnee shrugged and held his
hands palm up in front of his chest. 'I
was sneaking into Chucho's to get me a
drink and when I walked in I heard the
marshal's voice. I had a run-in with him

night 'fore last and I spent the night in jail. I just didn't want to see him again so damn' soon. Sorry about spooking you like that.'

The frown melted from the gunman's face. 'Hell, that's all right. All of us have had trouble with the law. Forget it.'

'You reckon the marshal is going to stay in there very long?' Shawnee asked with concern.

'Naw, he just come by to let us know he's still around. Hell, I don't know what him and his one deputy are goin' to do anyway,' the gunman added dismissively. 'I gotta go take a leak.'

'You go on,' Shawnee whispered. 'I'll just go back in and listen. Maybe the marshal's already left.'

The gunman walked to the outhouse. Shawnee opened the back door carefully and slipped back in. He heard the marshal say, 'Have a good evening and stay out of trouble,' as he left.

Another of Slatter's men said, 'What's he goin' to do about us bein' here anyway? They's just two'a them.'

Slatter turned and looked at the man. 'Don't underestimate that little greaser,' he cautioned. 'He's still alive wearing a badge in this place, he must handle himself pretty damn' good when it gets down to the nut-cutting.'

Slatter turned in his chair and yelled, 'Chooch! Where in hell are them girls? We got to have some girls in here!'

'My man is rounding them up now,' Chucho replied. 'They did not know you were coming or they would have been here already, waiting for you when you rode in.'

Shawnee almost laughed at Chucho's false earnestness. He knew the girls had fled at the mention of Slatter's name.

Slatter's man came in through the back door and Shawnee walked into the main room with him.

'Who the hell is that, Morgan?' Slatter demanded.

Morgan said, 'He came in the back door and was hiding from the marshal. He scared shit outta me when I went back there.'

157

Shawnee said, 'And he scared the shit outta me when he went for his gun. I thought I was a dead man.'

Slatter chuckled and asked, 'What's your name?'

Shawnee smiled and said, 'I go by John Jones.'

'You didn't want to see the marshal?'

'Hell no!' Shawnee said. 'I got a little drunk a couple of nights ago and he tossed me in that roach nest of a jail. I want to stay away from him as far as I can get.'

Shawnee stole a glance at Chucho. Chucho made no sign of recognition and busied himself stacking clean glasses.

'Sit down and have a drink, Jones,' Slatter said. 'My name is Finn Slatter. You've met Morgan. These fellows here are Williams, Helms and Kammadiener.'

'Kammadiener?' Shawnee asked.

Slatter chuckled and looked at Kammadiener. 'Yeah, I know. We just call him Kraut. It's easier to say.'

'Howdy fellows,' Shawnee said.

The three nodded uninterestedly and

turned their attention back to their drinks.

Shawnee sat down and Slatter poured a shot of tequila for him. Shawnee picked up the glass and saluted Slatter, said, 'Much obliged,' and tossed the fiery liquid down.

Shawnee wiped his mouth and asked, 'Where you fellows from?'

'We're from here and there,' Slatter answered. 'Kind of hard to claim a home town.' He looked at his companions. 'We been run out of damn near every county in Texas.'

His companions laughed heartily.

Shawnee joined in the laughter. 'That's one hell of a lot of counties,' he commented.

'Well, we ain't exactly welcome just about any place we go,' Slatter said.

'Sounds like you fellows travel around having a good time,' Shawnee said. 'What line of work you in?'

Williams and Helms laughed. Kammadiener grinned and Morgan looked at Slatter with his eyebrows raised.

Slatter leaned back and looked at the ceiling as if thinking about his reply. 'You might say,' he muttered, 'we're in the money-transfer bidness.'

His men laughed again. Helms poked Williams in the ribs.

Shawnee nodded and said, 'You must be well known in banking circles.'

'You got that right!' Morgan said, laughing.

'Well, I reckon I don't need to know any more than that,' Shawnee said. 'After all, I don't want to pry.'

Slatter slapped Shawnee on the shoulder. 'You're a pretty good fellow, Jones. Have another drink!'

'Don't mind if I do,' Shawnee replied.

While Slatter poured another shot of tequila, Shawnee asked, 'Where you fellows heading from here?'

'Why do you ask?' Slatter asked, suddenly serious.

Shawnee looked at him in surprise. 'I was just making conversation. I didn't mean nothing by it.'

'That marshal asked the same thing

'fore he left,' Slatter growled. 'I don't like law dogs knowin' my bidness.'

'I don't blame you a bit,' Shawnee said. 'I figure you'd rather surprise 'em.'

The gang leader looked at Shawnee as if surprised himself, then broke into laughter. 'Hell yes, you got that right!' he guffawed.

His men joined him in laughter.

Slatter leaned across the table and spoke in a low voice. 'We're goin' upriver. And since there ain't no law where we're goin,' I can tell you. It's a place called La Perdida.'

Shawnee looked blank. 'I never even heard of it. Is it new?'

'Nope,' Slatter answered smugly. 'It's been there for a while. Most honest folk don't know about it and those that do don't care nothin' about goin' there.'

Shawnee threw back his head and laughed heartily. 'You fellows are a caution if I ever saw one,' he chuckled.

'Anyway,' Slatter grunted. 'We got some bidness up there we got to see about.'

'If that damn frog-eater knows what

161

the hell's he's talkin' about,' Morgan interjected.

'Well, my old friend,' Slatter said in a conciliatory tone, 'we'll listen to what he has to say, then we'll decide.'

Shawnee wrinkled his brow and said, 'Friend of yours eats frogs, does he?'

'Oh hell!' Slatter spat. 'The fellow's name is Kennebec, which is a French name and Morgan there doesn't trust nobody that's French or even sounds like it. The French are supposed to enjoy eating frogs' legs, among other things.'

Except for Morgan, the men laughed.

'Don't trust them damn' frog-eaters,' Morgan mumbled.

'What time is all this happening?' Shawnee asked no one in particular. 'I'm going to have to show up at home or the old lady is going to get plumb pissed. She's already about to cut my throat over gettin' thrown in the hoose-gow.'

'What time is it, Chooch?' Slatter roared.

'It is almost ten o'clock, *señor*,' Chucho answered from behind the bar.

'Oh hell, I'm in trouble,' Shawnee said, getting to his feet. 'I'm going to have to get outta here 'fore those girls show up anyways.'

'I hate to see you go, Jones,' Slatter said. 'But if you got a happy home, you better keep it that way.'

'You're plumb right 'bout that,' Shawnee chuckled. 'I don't need no more trouble, 'specially the kind that makes noise in my ear when I get in bed at night.'

Morgan strolled to the cantina front door and looked out. He turned and said, 'That deputy is across the street watching this place. You better go out the back, Jones.'

'Damn. I appreciate that, Morgan. Thanks. Goodnight Mr Slatter, nice to have made your acquaintance.' To the other men he said, 'So long fellows, good luck on your trip.'

He sauntered out the back door and strode hurriedly down the alley. He made his way into the next block then cut between two buildings on to the main street. He looked carefully back towards the cantina, then walked across the street to the marshal's office.

When Shawnee came through the door, Gutierrez looked up expectantly.

'So what did you learn?' the marshal said.

'They are going to La Perdida,' Shawnee said, almost breathlessly. 'And danged if they ain't going there to visit the very man I'm going after, Marsh Kennebec!'

'What?' the marshal asked. '*Que providencia*!'

'I suspect,' Shawnee went on, 'Kennebec found a robbery target in Mexico when he was there. The law back there knows he was in Mexico, but they don't know where he went and what he was doing. It could be he saw something involving a lot of cash and looked easy. What the law did not know was that he somehow got hold of Slatter. It must be a big job because there's several

164

ways to split the proceeds.'

'I want to warn the people at the target first, wherever it is,' Gutierrez said. 'But if you kill Kennebec, that may stop the whole thing. Was there any hint as to what the job was to be?'

'None,' Shawnee answered. 'I pressed about as much as I could.'

'They are meeting in La Perdida. That is a hard place to reach,' Gutierrez said. 'Why meet there unless they are going on upriver for the job. There is nothing anywhere near the Rio Grande across from La Perdida. Maybe they go to El Paso?'

'Anything's possible,' Shawnee said. 'I've got to ponder this.'

'You thinking about going with them, and get close to Kennebec, then killing him?' Gutierrez asked.

'Something like that,' Shawnee said.

Booted footsteps sounded on the boardwalk outside. The door swung open and a man stepped through. He was wearing a white hat, dark-cotton shirt, denims and boots. He also wore a black leather vest to which was affixed the star of a Texas Ranger. An ivory-handled six-shooter rode on his right hip.

The Ranger looked at the marshal. 'You Gutierrez?'

'Yes, I am,' the marshal answered.

The Ranger reached into his shirt pocket and drew out a paper document. He unfolded it and handed it to Gutierrez.

The marshal held the paper close to the lantern and scanned it quickly.

'That's a warrant for the arrest of Finn Slatter and his gang. My name's Lou Rigler. They held up the Brewster bank downriver and killed a peace officer. I understand the gang is in town and I need your help to arrest them.'

Shawnee and Gutierrez looked at one another. They might not live to see another sunrise.

12

The marshal walked casually down the street to where Cruz stood, watching the activity at Chucho's cantina. He spoke with a low voice in Spanish, 'Don't ask questions. Just come back to the office. And don't look back at the cantina.'

Gutierrez turned and sauntered back toward the jail. Cruz fell in behind him without saying a word. Morgan stood in the cantina doorway and watched them. He turned to Slatter and said, 'The marshal just came and got his boy. They went back to the jail.'

'Were they in a hurry?' Slatter asked, suddenly sober.

'Naw, din't seem to be. Acting like they's out for a Sunday stroll,' Morgan replied.

Slatter went to the door and peered into the darkness. 'See anybody else out there?'

'Naw,' Morgan said. 'They's nobody on the street.'

Slatter returned to his chair and said, 'Chooch! Where in hell are those women?'

'They are coming, they are coming,' Chucho assured him.

At the jail, Gutierrez, Cruz, Shawnee and Rigler sat in a tight circle and planned their arrest of the Slatter gang. They discussed the cantina and its layout, the back door, the alley in back, the firearms each man wore and his position in the cantina when Shawnee left.

'We can't let any of them get past us and get to the stable where their horses are,' Gutierrez said.

Rigler held up an index finger. 'I took care of that before I came here,' he said. 'I stopped at the stable first and the stable boy and I relocated their horses. The stable boy will be in hiding so he won't get hurt.'

'Good thinking,' Gutierrez said.

After fifteen minutes of discussion, Rigler laid it out. 'Lanigan and Cruz will go to the back of the cantina and enter through the back door. When they are in place, the marshal and I will enter the front door with weapons drawn and order the gang to surrender. When I tell them to surrender, Cruz and Lanigan will enter the room from the other side and order hands up. If they refuse to put their hands up, shoot to kill. Any questions?'

There were no questions. Cruz and Lanigan went out the front door and across the street. They were too far away from the cantina and the street was too dark for anyone to see and identify them there. They edged between two buildings and into the alley. Gutierrez and Rigler would leave through the back door of the jail and use the buildings on that side of the street for cover. They would emerge from behind the general store and the saddlers, cross the street directly to the cantina's front door and walk in without warning.

Cruz and Shawnee were three buildings away from the cantina when a wagon pulled to a stop at the back door and started unloading whores. Lanigan and Cruz, stunned, stopped dead still. It was too late to stop them, the door was open and the girls were filing in. The presence of the *putas* horribly complicated things, since they would be in the line of fire. There was nothing they could do but carry through with the plan.

The wagon driver stepped down and entered the back door behind the girls, probably eager to get his reward, more than likely a bottle of tequila or pulque.

Cruz and Shawnee exchanged glances, pulled their weapons and slipped through the open back door. They entered silently and pressed themselves against the wall of the short hallway.

Shawnee felt the excitement in his stomach as he always did when facing a certain life or death battle, his nerves tingling. He loved the sensation but he hated having to face death or kill someone else to feel it.

He heard the swinging doors burst open and Rigler cry out, 'You're under arrest, get your hands up!'

It was time to move.

Shawnee and Cruz stepped around the corner and shouted, as one, 'hands up.' Five faces swivelled from the front door in unison and gaped at them. Helms and Williams reached for their holsters. Shawnee fired from the hip and Helms bucked backward to the floor. The remaining four men had their pistols out and were firing. Smoke filled the air, obscuring vision. The whores screamed and tried to take cover under the tables. One of them took a bullet and fell. Shawnee was vaguely aware of Cruz beside him firing rapidly.

Suddenly out of the smoke a strange shape materialized. It was one of Slatter's men pushing a whore in front of him. She was screaming at the top of her lungs. The man shoved the girl into Shawnee and then fired his pistol into her back. Shawnee felt an impact on his chest as the girl fell against him, driving him backward. He stumbled and fell, the girl atop him. He rolled her off like a sack of wheat and fired at the shape of the man running for the back door. Shawnee was struggling to his feet when Williams staggered out of the smoke directly toward him. Shawnee raised his weapon but Williams's eyes were blank and a gout of blood covered his chest. Williams stumbled past Shawnee and fell face downward.

Shawnee got to his feet and stepped over a body. It was Cruz. He had been hit in the chest and was motionless. Shawnee groped his way through the hallway to the back door. No one was there. The man who had pushed the girl into him had escaped. He turned and looked back. Slatter was on his knees firing at someone; Shawnee could not see who. Slatter had been hit but was still fighting. Shawnee whipped around and dived out the back door. Far down the alley he caught a glimpse of a running figure as it passed a lighted window. He broke into a run after it.

The figure fled down the street and into the livery stable. Shawnee followed hard, gasping for air. As he approached the building, he heard loud cursing. The fugitive had just discovered his horse was not in the stable. Shawnee stopped outside the door. A solitary kerosene lamp feebly lit a small area of the stable. Shawnee stopped short of the pool of light and stayed in the shadows to take stock. He heard boots on wood and recognized the sound as someone climbing a ladder. The Slatter henchman was climbing into the barn's loft. Shawnee stood in the darkness listening for any tell-tale noises. There was silence except for an occasional sound of one of the horses moving in its stall. There were no more shots from the direction of the cantina.

Shawnee could not let this man escape. If the henchman got to La Perdida, he could identify Shawnee to the band of cutthroats infesting that unhappy place and cut his mission short. He backtracked out of the barn to the outside. He wouldn't be able to traverse that dim pool of light without being seen. He remembered the other door at the rear of the barn which would allow him access inside the building under the loft where the brigand had taken refuge. He reloaded his pistol by feel and walked around the barn. He reached the back door and paused. Opening the door would be noisy and would invite a volley of blind shots. Then he thought of a diversion. He whistled softly to Candy, the whistle he used to summon her when she was grazing in a field. Inside the stable, Candy snorted, whinnied and kicked at the walls of her stall in her impatience to answer. Shawnee pulled the door open and entered the darkened stable.

No shots. His plan had worked.

Shawnee crept forward quietly, a half-step at a time, to get the area under the hiding-place between himself and the lantern's light. He found a small corn crib behind him. He picked up a corn cob carefully so the dried shuck did not crackle too loudly and tossed it across the stable. It hit a wall with a satisfying thump and shuffling noises above him indicated that his quarry was still up there. Shawnee saw what he was looking for: a thin sifting of dust falling from the loft between boards. He raised his pistol and fired four times. With a cry of pain, a body slipped out of the loft and fell heavily to the floor.

The body did not move so Shawnee got to the lantern, picked it up and approached the body. It was Morgan; he lay with his eyes open, staring toward the sky, seeing nothing.

★ ★ ★

When the sun came up, Finn Slatter and his men were dead. Deputy Marshal Cruz was dead, two whores were dead and one was wounded but expected to recover, Marshal Gutierrez was wounded in the fleshy part of his hip and Ranger Lew Rigler was unscathed. Shawnee Lanigan escaped without a scratch as well. After Gutierrez got himself sewn up by the veterinarian, who doubled as the town doctor, he filled out a form and gave it to Shawnee who took it to the bank and cashed it for forty dollars. Shawnee stayed in town long enough to attend Cruz's funeral and then took his leave.

The marshal was rapidly becoming a legend as the result of the cantina gunfight and, of course, Ranger Rigler was already a legend. Chucho left things in the cantina pretty much as they were when the gunfight ended. He found the locals and the travellers to be fascinated by violent death so he didn't bother to repair the bullet holes and he left the bloodstains on the floor so the curious could gawk at them and buy his beer and tequila while he recounted a greatly embellished, shot by shot, version of the entire gunfight.

Gutierrez bid a fond *adios* to Shawnee because he was certain his new friend was going to a sure death. Lanigan rode Candy out of town, with Escamillo in tow, and headed upriver toward whatever fate had decreed.

13

Shawnee had no more than a vague idea of the distance from Presidio to La Perdida, only that it was over fifty miles. However, a fifty-mile trek in the Chihuahuan desert was not to be taken lightly and he prepared for it. A short distance from the river the landscape was populated by the desert tarantula, the large scorpions known as vinegaroons, and giant centipedes. At night, the snakes that avoided the daytime sun crept about, looking for tasty treats such as salamanders, geckos and the indiscreet mouse. The careful traveler learned early on to empty unwelcome visitors out of his boots before putting them on in the morning. The floral denizens were not attractive, being largely creosote bush, yucca, mesquite, acacia and tarbush.

In the afternoon of the fourth day on

the trail, Shawnee sighted the notorious town. He rode up the dusty main street and straight to the only building labelled, in crude hand-lettering, SALOON. He hitched Candy and Escamillo outside, strolled into the rustic establishment to the stares of a pair of locals and ordered a beer. The beer tasted absolutely terrible but Shawnee choked it down in the interests of establishing friendly relations with the bartender, who, as Shawnee learned, was called 'Lop' because of his mutilated ear.

'Did I understand correctly,' Shawnee said to the bartender, 'that you are called 'Lop'?'

'Thass right,' the unfortunate man said. 'I can't figure out why, but thass what they call me.'

Shawnee kept a straight face because he wasn't sure whether the bartender was serious or merely ribbing a stranger, and said, 'I can't either.'

'You can't what?' Lop asked.

'I can't figure out why they call you 'Lop',' Shawnee answered.

'Who calls me 'Lop'?' Lop asked.

Shawnee took a deep breath and said, 'You told me everybody calls you 'Lop'.'

'Sure I did!' Lop said somewhat indignantly. 'Thass what they call me.'

Shawnee extricated himself from the mentally confused Lop and casually addressed the only other person standing at the bar.

'You happen to know Marsh Kennebec?' he asked.

'Yeah,' the man said. 'Don't know him well, just when I see 'im, I know it's Marsh Kennebec.'

'Know where I might find him?'

The man scrunched up his eyes, thinking. 'I think he lives in one of those shacks on the north side of town.'

The man turned to his beer as if uninterested in further conversation. Shawnee drained the last of his beer and walked back outside.

He located a stable of sorts, actually a barn, where he could board his animals at a cost of a dollar a day for both. When Shawnee objected to the excessive price, the gape-mouthed young man in charge shrugged his shoulders and said, 'That's what Mr Crown told me to charge, fifty cents an animal a night.'

'Who in hell is Crown?' Shawnee asked rudely.

'Who is Crown!' the boy almost shouted. 'You don't know shit, do ya? He's the man what owns this whole place. He's the king.'

Shawnee walked away, leaving the boy chuckling to himself.

There were few buildings in La Perdida. The largest and the one in best repair was the saloon. There was a store where foodstuff was sold in air-tights for outrageous prices. There was a gun-smith and a small building marked 'Crown Office'. One place marked 'Tamales' was run by a Mexican gentleman and his wife. There was a hotel of sorts, actually an old home converted to a dormitory-style arrangement for temporary residents.

Shawnee investigated the hotel and rented a cot for the night. The proprietor informed him the rent included the cot only and if he wanted bedding, he'd have to supply it himself. He located his cot in a small room with three other cots. I figure I can handle one night anyway, he thought.

From the proprietor, Shawnee learned who Hiram Crown was. He had rebuilt a deserted ghost town near a fresh-water spring and called it La Perdida. It became a refuge for fugitives from justice, murderers, swindlers, bank robbers and miscreants of all stripes. When the law mounted enough men to attempt a raid on La Perdida to capture a specific fugitive, they were in for a gunfight or for seeing the population fade away into the desert and cross the border into Mexico. Since an armed force of some size was required to face down the abundance of guns represented by those infesting the town, lawmen tried to ignore it so far as possible. So by tacit agreement, only the perpetrators of the most egregious crimes weren't safe in La Perdida.

He made additional inquiries and

learned where Marsh Kennebec lived. The place, a small adobe, was about a quarter-mile up the road. He considered getting Candy out of the stable but decided to walk instead, reasoning he needed to get the kinks out after four days in the saddle.

When he knocked at the door, a young girl, about fifteen or sixteen, opened it. She had the customary dark eyes and raven hair; she wore a thin shift and her figure was well filled out.

'Que?' she said, looking at him suspiciously.

'Marsh Kennebec?' he answered.

The girl turned and called, 'Marsh?'

In a few moments, Marsh Kennebec shuffled to the door. Shawnee recognized him immediately from Little Brick's description. His dark hair hung down on both sides of his head, greasily framing his face. The hair had started turning white at a spot on the forehead and had grown long resembling the stripe on a skunk's back. A knife scar on his lower lip puckered and drew the lip down so the lower teeth could never be entirely concealed. His teeth were gapped and brown-stained. Lanigan shuddered at the thought of what Betsy Kincaid's last moments must have been like, with such a vile creature assaulting her.

Kennebec looked at Shawnee and said, 'Who in hell are you and what do you want?'

'My name is John Jones and I'm here to deliver a message,' Shawnee responded.

'Who from?' Kennebec growled, frowning suspiciously. Shawnee smelled liquor on his breath.

'From Finn Slatter,' Shawnee answered.

The frown disappeared. 'Come in,' Kennebec said and stood aside.

Kennebec motioned his guest to a table holding a tequila bottle and a glass. He said something to the girl and she produced another glass. Kennebec poured two drinks without asking and shoved one over in front of Shawnee, tossed down his own drink, wiped his mouth with his sleeve and leaned back.

'Whass ol' Finn have to say?' he asked, smiling, or at least it looked like a smile.

'He said he won't be able to come to La Perdida,' Shawnee answered.

Kennebec sat up straight. 'Why the hell not?' he demanded.

'He took the big jump,' Shawnee said without emotion.

Kennebec's mouth fell open forming an even more nightmarish and grotesque countenance than Shawnee could have imagined. Kennebec stared at Shawnee for a full five seconds. Then he brought his fist crashing down on the table, knocking over the tequila bottle. He roared, 'Damn it to hell!'

Shawnee noticed that the girl looked frightened. She backed out of the room.

'What the hell happened?' Kennebec demanded.

Shawnee leaned forward and put on a serious mien. 'He got surprised by a Texas Ranger, the Presidio town marshal and a deputy. He and his men were sitting in a cantina drinking and some girls had just come in. They were having a high old time and all of a sudden, that ranger and the marshal busted through the front door and started shooting. At the same time, a deputy come in the back door with two guns blazing. By the time the smoke cleared, Slatter's men were dead and he was dying. And the deputy marshal and a couple of the girls were dead.'

'When did he tell you about coming to see me?' Slatter asked.

'The night before he died; we were drinking together and he told me he was going to cook up something with you. He didn't say what. The next day I was heading for the cantina when the shooting started. When it stopped, I went in and saw Finn lying on the floor. He raised up on one elbow and I went over and told him to hold on, we'd get a sawbones and he said it warn't no use, he was dying. He pulled me down to his ear and his voice was kind of gurgly. He said, 'Tell Kennebec I can't make it this time and give him my regrets.' Then he just kind of laid back and all the air went out of him.

'Well sir, I looked around at all that blood and I said to myself, 'let's get the hell out of here'. And I did.' Shawnee paused for a moment, then said, 'Sorry to bring you bad news, but I figured it'd be best you knew.'

Kennebec had been staring at the table top during Shawnee's narrative. He looked up and said, 'I 'preciate it. What's your name? Jones? Yeah, I appreciate you coming all the way up here to let me know.'

'To tell you the truth, things were getting a little warm for me in Texas,' Shawnee said with a sly grin. 'I figured I'd come down here and let it cool off for a bit.'

Shawnee got up to go and Kennebec walked him to the door.

Shawnee said, 'If you ever need another hand or a gun, let me know.'

Kennebec smiled his bizarre smile revealing his lower teeth and said, 'I'll do that.'

Shawnee knew he wouldn't be able to handle Kennebec, his horse and Escamillo on the return trip, so he had to pare down a bit. He asked the stable boy if he knew of anyone needing a *burro*. The stable boy said he did and arranged for his friend Jorge to get together with Shawnee. Jorge was poor and had no money for buying a *burro* so Shawnee sold the animal to him for a half-dollar. The boy was ecstatic and went away in high spirits.

Shawnee then put together the supplies he thought he'd need to get himself, Kennebec and their two horses back to Presidio. Shawnee reasoned if he could get the fugitive into the jail at Presidio, he could make arrangements with his client by telegraph to have Kennebec escorted back to Eagle Pass. That, at least, was his plan; a plan that included a great many 'ifs' and was fraught with difficulty and danger. It would be easier just to kill Kennebec in the night and scurry back to civilization before the deed was discovered, but he would try to play it the legal way.

With his preparations made, Shawnee went to the hotel and lay down on his cot to take a nap. It would be the last sleep he would get until they reached Presidio. He drifted off quickly and when he awoke, the sun was setting.

He got up, moseyed down the street to the tamale place and had supper. Then he visited the stable, got Candy and loaded his gear on to her. From one saddle-bag he took a substantial length of leather thong, cut two shorter lengths from it and stuffed them into a pocket. He then climbed into the saddle and started back toward Kennebec's adobe. As he passed the saloon, he had an idea and pulled up. He hitched the horse in front, went to the door and peered inside. His hunch paid off. Kennebec was sitting at a table with what appeared to be a drover. Shawnee changed his plan instantly. Here, he wouldn't have the girl to deal with and he could wait until his quarry had a few drinks or several, then waylay him on his way home.

Shawnee sauntered into the saloon and up to the bar. He ordered a beer from Lop, then turned casually and glanced at the other drinkers. Kennebec caught Shawnee's eye. Shawnee nodded in greeting and, when he got his beer, walked over to Kennebec's table and sat down.

Kennebec said, 'I see you're still around, Jones.'

Shawnee smiled and replied, 'This is a good place to go to ground. I'll nest here until the money gets low, then I'm on the trail again. That is, unless I find gainful employment hereabouts.'

Kennebec laughed. 'That ain't too likely. Oh, by the way, this fellow here is Russ Snelgar. Russ, this is John Jones. He's the one come to tell me Finn Slatter got ambushed.'

Shawnee shook hands with Snelgar and his breath caught in his throat. He concentrated on keeping emotion off his face while his stomach became uneasy. *Damn! I know that name. Is this the same person?* Shawnee thought.

Snelgar shook hands, glancing at Shawnee only briefly before returning to his drink without giving a sign of recognition. Shawnee turned the conversation to other things.

'I've noticed a few women scattered around here, Marsh,' Shawnee said. 'Are there any who accommodate lonely cowboys?'

'Oh sure,' Kennebec said. 'There's old Gummy Gertie. She doesn't have a tooth in her head and she's about eighty, but it's better'n nothing.'

'That ain't too inviting,' Shawnee said, sceptically.

Snelgar suddenly turned and looked at him intently.

Oh hell, Shawnee thought. *He's remembered who I am.*

'Where do you take a leak around here?' Shawnee asked.

Kennebec pointed at a door in the back of the saloon. 'Go out that door and the privy is on your right. If it stinks too bad in there for you, just go past the privy and whip it out. We don't stand on ceremony 'round here.'

Shawnee laughed heartily and walked to the door. He thought he could feel Snelgar's eyes on the back of his neck. He went through the door and walked quickly to the left. He rounded the building's corner, stopped and peered around the corner at the back of the building.

Shawnee's mind was racing. Snelgar was a member of a gang he helped put behind bars ten years before. If Snelgar remembered him, it could cost him his life.

In moments, a figure emerged from the back door and walked toward the privy, and Shawnee got his answer. In the light from the open doorway, Shawnee saw that a pistol was in the man's right hand.

It was Snelgar.

14

Shawnee had to deal with Snelgar and do it quietly. He turned and walked briskly into the darkness. There were two outbuildings behind the stable and Shawnee headed for them. He reached the first one and circled it, stopping on the backside. He took off his hat and peered around the corner. Snelgar was following.

Good! Shawnee thought. *I hope he didn't say anything to Kennebec about me.*

Shawnee flattened himself against the shack's wall and waited. In moments, he heard hurried footsteps. Snelgar was coming up on his left, so he moved to the right and slipped around the next corner. He heard Snelgar approach, pause then spring suddenly.

'Shit!' Snelgar spat when he saw no one.

Shawnee edged on around the shack and around another corner. He peeked around the next corner and saw Snelgar standing and peering into the darkness toward the other shack. Snelgar, muttering, edged toward the other shack. Shawnee pulled his hunting knife from its sheath and tiptoed toward Snelgar. He would grab the man from behind, clap his left hand over Snelgar's mouth and shove the knife into his right kidney. But just as he reached out, Snelgar swiveled around.

As Snelgar grunted and swung around to bring his pistol to bear, Shawnee swung the knife. The point caught Snelgar in the right forearm. Snelgar cried out and the six-gun dropped from his hand. Shawnee pressed the attack, moving forward, left hand reaching for his target's face with his knife held to his side, elbow bent, ready to thrust. Shawnee thrust toward Snelgar's stomach but the outlaw jumped back with surprising agility and pulled his own knife with his left hand.

Snelgar extended his left arm and held the knife toward Shawnee, holding his injured right arm against his stomach.

Good, Shawnee thought. *That's just what I wanted.* Snelgar couldn't reach him with a thrust without moving his feet. Shawnee extended his left hand toward his opponent's face and held the knife in his right, elbow bent, at the height of his lowest rib. Snelgar slashed clumsily at Shawnee's left hand, a move easily avoided. Shawnee stuck his hand out again, feinting at Snelgar's face, then dropping it toward the man's stomach. Snelgar slashed again, a broad sweeping stroke. At that moment, as Snelgar's knife pointed away from him, Shawnee took one step with his right foot and at the same time, thrust the knife into Snelgar's chest and immediately retracted it.

Snelgar looked at Shawnee in confusion, realized he had been badly wounded, and cried out. He charged slashing wildly. Shawnee parried a slash and dodged aside and, as Snelgar's momentum carried him past, thrust his knife between his ribs. Snelgar stopped and swayed uncertainly. Shawnee heard the outlaw's breath coming in rattles as blood from his lungs filled his throat. The knife dropped from his left hand, he staggered slightly then his knees folded and he fell without a sound.

Shawnee wiped his knife on Snelgar's shirt, sheathed it, then took Snelgar by the collar and dragged him into the shack. The shack appeared to be used for storage and Shawnee hoped the body would not be found for hours. He picked up his hat and returned to the cantina. He entered through the back door and scanned the room. He saw Kennebec sitting alone at a table, ordered a drink and carried it to the table. As he sat down, Kennebec looked up at him, frowning.

'Where in hell you been?' Kennebec asked.

'I had to take a dump and that damned privy was too filthy for me,'

Shawnee replied. 'I walked up to the house where I rented a cot.'

'You see Snelgar?'

Without changing expression, Shawnee replied he had not and Kennebec shrugged his shoulders.

'I'm ready to get out of here,' Kennebec said. 'I'm headin' back to the 'dobe.'

'I'll walk out with you,' Shawnee said.

The two men walked out of the cantina and mounted their horses. They moved at a slow walk up the street.

'What's all that gear you got loaded on there?' Kennebec asked, looking at the supplies Shawnee had loaded.

'It's stuff I'm taking back to the hotel so I can keep my eye on it,' Shawnee replied.

'Why don't you come out to the 'dobe and have a drink of my stuff,' Kennebec asked. 'It's better'n that horse piss old Lop serves up.'

'Sure, it's too early to turn in. Besides, I'd like to find out if that gal of yours has a sister.'

Kennebec grinned. 'She's something,' ain't she? Nice body for a fifteen-year-old. Cooks pretty good too. But she's getting a little long in the tooth for me. Have to trade her in pretty soon for a younger one.'

Shawnee stifled an impulse to call his companion a filthy name and chuckled instead. 'She's still got a lotta good left in her,' he said. 'Somebody might make you a good deal on the trade.'

Kennebec chuckled wickedly.

They passed by the last buildings at the edge of town into the darkness. Shawnee looked back at his goods and said, 'What the hell? Hold it a minute, Marsh.'

He reined his horse to a stop and dismounted. He walked around the horse and started tugging at the straps holding his goods. He reached into the pack and grasped the slung shot he had hidden there, shoving it into his belt. He muttered to himself and uttered an occasional 'damn'.

Kennebec dismounted and walked over to him saying, 'Need a hand?' As he spoke, Shawnee hit him in the head with the slung shot, felling him immediately. He wasn't quite unconscious so Shawnee hit him again. Shawnee turned him over on his stomach, pulled his arms behind him and tied them together with a length of leather thong. When Kennebec started waking up and groaning, Shawnee pulled him to his feet and stood him beside his horse. He hoisted the barely conscious man up onto the horse's back, face down, draped over his own saddle. Shawnee tied a long leather thong around Kennebec's ankles, ran it under the horse, looped it around the saddle horn and tied it around his prisoner's neck. As Shawnee took the reins of Kennebec's horse and climbed back into his own saddle, he heard horses approaching up the road from town. With Kennebec in tow, he set off at a gallop toward the south-east.

Shawnee looked back and saw that

someone was following. In the darkness he wasn't sure how many, but there was enough moonlight for him to make out pursuers. He cursed his luck and the fact that he had not killed Kennebec and taken his scalp instead of trying to return him to the bar of justice.

The chase was a short one. Candy had never been a fast horse and Shawnee was further hampered by having to keep Kennebec's horse in tow. He heard a horse close behind him but kept pressing onwards. He was aware that horses were on either side of him when someone shouted, 'Stop or I'll shoot.' He looked and the man was only feet away. He knew he was beaten and reined Candy to a halt.

* * *

Shawnee awoke from a fitful sleep the next morning to find himself in a dark room. A bit of light showed under the room's one door. He lay on the rude cot and took stock. One eye was swollen. Both lips were split and sore and a couple of teeth were loose. His stomach was sore from Kennebec's fist and his head hurt. He wondered why he was still alive.

There was noise at the door and it swung open. A grinning cowboy asked, 'You ready to go?'

'Go where?' Shawnee asked, squinting into the light.

'To your trial,' the cowboy said with surprise. 'Don't you know about La Perdida? We always put people on trial 'fore we hang 'em. Come on, you can take a leak, then we got to go down to the cantina.'

*   *   *

Shawnee Lanigan looked around the room at the worst bunch of cutthroats, thieves, murderers and highwaymen he had ever seen in one place in his life. What was worse, they all wanted his blood. He was in a tight spot and he knew he couldn't kill enough of them to make an escape so he was going to have to be pretty damned clever.

Shawnee was starting to think: this pitiful spot, which wasn't even on any map, that he thought would be the end of Kennebec's trail, would be the end of his own instead. He had caught Kennebec but before he could get his prey out of town, he had been bushwhacked by a veritable phalanx of gunmen, and if he didn't survive this trial, who would know? It was then that he remembered the little boy who had never mourned his mother and father and the pain he would suffer the rest of his life. Suddenly, the noise in the room faded and the memory of that night and his own childhood agony came pouring back into his consciousness. He was isolated in darkness, grief overwhelmed him and he cried out.

'What the hell's wrong with you?' The man who had escorted him peered into his face, his brow wrinkled.

The noise, the stink and the ugly world around him returned. Shawnee looked around the room at his tormentors as if seeing them for the first time. Knowing it was going to take everything he had to live through what was coming, he began to gather his resolve.

Shawnee sat in a chair in the center of the room, the main salon of the Horned Toad saloon, center of social life and official proceedings in La Perdida. Hiram Crown sat behind a big table against the north wall. Crown was a big, broad-shouldered man dressed as a gentleman. His shoes were shined and a gold chain with a fob dangled from a pocket of his vest.

The toughs, ex-convicts, murderers and scum of the earth representing La Perdida's finest citizens sat in the available chairs, stood around the walls on both sides or leaned against the bar. It was to be a trial, a trial where the worst criminals in Texas and Mexico would determine his fate.

Shawnee saw his Colt Model 1878 .44 on the table in front of Crown. Beside it was his Winchester and his hunting knife. He wondered what they had done with Candy and his saddle.

The brutish Marsh Kennebec sat off to the left of Crown's table, his yellow eyes watching Lanigan, a sneer curling his upper lip even more than usual and, with his mutilated lower lip, his expression surpassed the grotesque. When someone close by said something funny to Kennebec, he looked around at the jokester and laughed, showing even more of his brown-stained teeth.

Hiram Crown pounded on the table with the butt of his pistol. When the laughing and chatter failed to stop immediately, he yelled, 'Shut the hell up!' The noise died away and Crown, grim-faced, looked around the room waiting for some highbinder to let slip a chuckle.

'Stay the hell quiet!' he added. Then he addressed the motley crowd as if it were a duly constituted jury of his prisoner's peers. 'This fellow you see here is called Shawnee Lanigan. He is a hired gun come to our town to get an upstanding citizen of La Perdida, our long-time friend, Marsh Kennebec, and take him back to Eagle Pass for trial. What we're going to do today is to decide what, under the laws of La Perdida, we are going to do with this fellow.'

Several men in the crowd roared, 'Hang 'im!'

Shawnee realized, with a trace of relief, that they had not found Snelgar's body.

Kennebec greeted the crowd's reaction with a nightmarish grimace that would have sent small children screaming for their mothers, but which his acquaintances recognized as a broad smile. He stood and accepted the plaudits of the crowd.

'Now wait a minute,' Crown responded in an authoritarian voice. 'You know as well as I do, anybody we hang in La Perdida has to have a fair trial first.'

The crowd roared with laughter.

Shawnee stood up, a fixed expression on his face, betraying neither anger nor fear. 'Do I get a chance to testify in my own behalf, Crown?' he shouted.

Crown looked surprised. 'Why, of course,' he replied, as if his feelings had been bruised by the question. 'You'll get your chance to tell your story and Marsh Kennebec will have a chance to question you. By the way, you will address me as 'Your Honour' or 'Judge Crown' or 'Your Worship' if you prefer. Understand?'

'Will I have the opportunity to question Kennebec, Your Honour?' Shawnee asked in a strong even voice without a hint of emotion.

'If our jury,' Crown said, his arm sweeping around the crowd lining the barroom, 'deems it necessary.'

More laughter.

'Court is in session,' Crown announced. 'There will be no whiskey or beer sold while court is in session. We're goin' to keep this damned trial civilized!'

Groans arose from the assemblage.

Crown frowned at the crowd then continued. 'The attorney for the pros-ecution will take the floor first and explain to us just what this Lanigan fellow did to him, or at least, tried to do.'

Kennebec sprang to his feet amidst the crowd's cheers and shook his clasped hands together above his head as if he were a box fighter celebrating a victory. He strutted around the floor acknowledging the admiration of his peers. He wore his pistol in a holster on his left side, butt forward, for a right-hand draw.

'There I was,' he started. 'Enjoying a quiet evening in La Perdida.'

There was a scattering of laughter.

'I played a little poker, drank a little whiskey, then decided to go home, say my prayers . . .'

There was general hilarity.

'And go to bed. But as I started home, this Lanigan fellow says he'll ride with me. And being neighborly, I asked him to go out to my place and have a drink and visit with my soul mate.'

Subdued chuckles.

'Then this bastard tricks me off my horse saying he has a problem with his saddle rigging and when I try to help 'im, he hits me with a sap. While I'm out, he ties me up and slings me across my own saddle and says, 'Keep quiet, Kennebec, and you'll live for a while. I'm takin' you back to Eagle Pass. If you squawk, I'll shove this pistol up your ass and blow your guts out'.'

Kennebec threw his hands in the air and said, 'What could I do? He got the jump on me, he's got a pistol under my chin. All I can do is go along and hope for the best.'

The crowd murmured in agreement.

'And off we go with me trying to breathe, trussed up like a turkey. We git a half-mile outside of town and I hear horses running. My old pal Tomer Paul suspected somethin' was up and he runs and tells the other fellows, and they come to the rescue.'

A bald-headed man with a fierce black beard stood up, shaking his arms over his head and grinning a snaggle-toothed grin. The assemblage cheered him loudly.

'Thank you, Tomer,' Kennebec said. 'I might say I would be happy to do the same for those fellows any time, any place. Anyways, Lanigan hears 'em comin' and he starts to gallop holdin' my horse's reins.'

'But the boys ride up on us and tell him to stop or they'll shoot him down like a dog and he got no choice but to drop his iron and stick his hands in the air. And that's what happened.'

The crowd chuckled appreciatively.

Someone in the crowd yelled, 'How come he was after your sweet little ass?'

More laughter.

'That's a good question,' Kennebec said smiling. 'A few weeks ago, I was on my way through Eagle Pass after transacting some business in Mexico . . .'

Chuckles, knowing hoots and rude noises rose from the audience.

' . . . and I decided to drop in on a fellow of my acquaintance, name of Ward Kincaid. It was somethin' over ten years ago when I last saw him. He was testifying at the trial that got me sent to the shit hole in Huntsville for ten years. I swore I'd get even with that son-of-a-bitch if I ever got out of prison, and I found myself in the town where he lived. Well, it warn't a bit of trouble to find out where this Kincaid lives so I drops by the house and puts a forty-five slug in 'im. Then I come on here to be with my friends. I reckon this Lanigan fellow here thought he'd pick up a nice reward for takin' me back to Eagle Pass, but my old friend Tomer crossed him up good.'

Kennebec turned and strutted back to his chair while the crowd roared its approval. Shouts of, 'Hang 'im,' could be heard from the more impatient of the jurors.

Crown held up his hand for silence and looked at Shawnee. 'It's your turn, Mr Lanigan.'

A few groans were voiced among the jury.

'Thank you, Judge Crown,' Lanigan said politely while Crown smiled and preened.

Shawnee paused for a moment to let silence return to the room, then started his defence.

'Everything Mr Kennebec said just now is true, everything except the part where I would shoot him up the ass. If I had shot him, it would have been between the eyes.'

Kennebec looked momentarily uncomfortable.

'So I can't say anything else he said was untrue.'

The crowd murmured.

'But his part of the truth doesn't quite cover it. The whole truth is what they look for in a courtroom and this court should be no different. So I'm going to tell you the rest of it and I don't have to lie. But if Mr Kennebec denies what I'm going to say, he will be lying.'

Kennebec looked serious and squirmed in his chair.

'Kennebec came to Eagle Pass and he went to where Ward Kincaid had bought a house for his wife. He had married her a couple of years after Kennebec's trial. She was the prettiest, sweetest thing you ever saw; dark hair, blue eyes that would make a man believe in God, and the most loving disposition you can imagine.'

'What's all this about that quim?' Kennebec shouted. 'What's that have to do with anything?'

There were loud mutterings of impatience in the crowd.

Crown banged his pistol on the table and the crowd quieted.

Lanigan went on. 'You didn't know they had a child, did you, Kennebec?'

Kennebec looked surprised.

'No, you didn't; because you never saw him. When Ward Kincaid saw you walking up to his front door, he told his little five-year-old son to stay with his mama and not come out no matter what. Even when you two exchanged loud words, and he called you by name, he and his mama didn't come out, but they were listening. When you shot his unarmed father in his own house, the boy's mama couldn't hold still anymore and she came in screaming and you tried to rape her. That little boy didn't come out but he heard his mother screaming. When you couldn't have your way and you shot that mother of that small boy in her own sitting room, he didn't come out, but he heard her die. If he had come out of hiding, he wouldn't be alive today to tell the story, would he, Kennebec?'

The crowd was silent. All heads were turned, looking at Kennebec, who was glaring at Lanigan with pure malevolence.

'You wanted revenge on Ward Kincaid because he sent you to prison. All these men,' Lanigan said, waving his hand around the room, 'understand that. Revenge is sweet. But why did you kill Betsy, who never even heard of you, the mother of a small child. Why did you kill her, Kennebec?'

Kennebec snarled, 'Because she was there and she saw me. I couldn't have no witness.'

'And because she fought you like a tiger when you tried to tear her clothes off and rape her. Isn't that true, Kennebec?'

Kennebec leaped to his feet. 'So what?' he rasped. 'She was married to that goody-goody. She had it coming.'

The crowd murmured again but its tone was different.

'And another thing, Kennebec,' Lanigan went on. 'You walked out the front door after you killed those two people and what did you see? You saw the little boy's dog. It was a big shaggy dog that liked everyone. He was just a mutt; the blood of three or four breeds ran through his veins and his coat was mulkety-colored and not very pretty. But he never met a stranger, liked everyone, and he probably ran up to you to be petted like he did with everyone because he didn't know about not trusting people. He ran right up to you and what did you do?'

Kennebeck looked at the floor.

'What did you do?' Lanigan roared.

Kennebeck didn't answer.

'You shot that dog!' Lanigan shouted. 'It wasn't enough that you orphaned that little boy and left scars on his soul that will last forever, *you shot that little boy's dog.*'

Lanigan looked around at the crowd. 'Any of you have a dog when you were a little boy? That dog loved you without question and you loved it. There was to be no comfort for that little boy after he saw his parents lying there in their own blood, because the creature that loved him almost as much as his parents was dead too.'

Lanigan was silent, listening to the murmurs in the room.

'Is that all you have to say, Lanigan?' Crown asked.

'One more small thing, Your Honour,' Shawnee replied.

He turned to Kennebec, who was squirming uncomfortably. Even he felt the changed mood among the *desparadoes* in the room.

'Tell us, Kennebec,' Shawnee went

214

on. 'You said Kincaid testified against you at your trial. Why were you on trial in the first place?'

Kennebec looked up at Lanigan and reached for his pistol. A large man standing beside him grabbed his arm and took the pistol.

'Don't like that question, Kennebec?' Shawnee almost shouted. 'The truth is, Ward Kincaid not only testified against you, he was the one who caught you in the act of the crime for which you went to prison for ten years. He caught you in a livery stable trying to rape a girl, didn't he?'

Kennebec said, 'What the hell, I was just having some fun with one of the locals.'

'That's right, you were,' Shawnee said. He paused for three full seconds. 'Ward Kincaid heard the screaming and he caught you with the girl after you had torn most of her clothes off and you had your pants down around your ankles and you were about to shove that filthy bone of yours into *a little nine-year-old girl.'*

There was a collective gasp from the crowd, followed by low murmuring.

'What the hell?' Kennebec growled. 'She was just a little white trash gal.'

'I rest my case, Judge Crown,' Shawnee said.

Crown stared at Kennebec for a long while before turning to the crowd.

'What say you?' he asked. 'Should we hang this fellow?'

There was a babble of voices from the crowd. 'Let 'em fight it out!' someone shouted.

A chorus of voices joined in. 'Yeah, make it a fair fight.'

Crown listened for a while then rapped on the table. 'The judgment of this court is these two men be taken outside and properly armed and be allowed to fight it out.'

Kennebec paled and his knees sagged. He yelled at Crown but his voice was drowned out in the excited babble of the crowd.

'Your honour,' Shawnee yelled. 'If I

win, can I have my weapons and my horse back and be allowed to leave?'

'Sure,' Crown said. 'You'll leave any cash money or other valuables here, but you can take your other goods with you.'

'Fair enough,' Shawnee said. He looked at Kennebec and grinned.

Crown stood up and added, 'The sentence is to be carried out immediately. Court's dismissed.' To the bartender he said, 'Lop, you can start selling whiskey again.'

Kennebec darted out of the room through the back door. Crown turned to one of his henchmen, a big cowboy wearing a black hat, and nodded toward the back door where Kennebec had disappeared. Black Hat strode across the room and out the back door. Shawnee picked up his knife and replaced it in its scabbard. He checked his pistol for a full cylinder and thrust it into its holster. He turned and walked through the doors with the murmuring crowd. The men stopped on the boardwalk and watched Shawnee step into the street. Some of the men looked about through the crowd and asked, 'Where's Kennebec?' In a few minutes, Black Hat came out the saloon door with a distraught-looking Kennebec in tow. Black Hat released Kennebec, shoving him off the boardwalk into the street.

Shawnee noticed that when Black Hat took his position beside his boss, Crown leaned over and whispered in his ear. Black Hat nodded, picked his way through the crowd and stopped behind Kennebec's rescuer, Tomer.

Kennebec looked at Shawnee, then straightened up and tried to put on a confident air. He walked with an exaggerated swagger into the street with a sneer on his face as if Lanigan wasn't worth his efforts. Someone in the crowd made a wisecrack and Kennebec stalked over to the edge of the street and started berating the wisecracker. Shawnee suspected the argument was a ruse. Kennebec was half-turned away, ostensibly arguing with the unknown tormentor. Shawnee watched his opponent's right elbow, which was barely showing. Suddenly the elbow disappeared as if he had extended his arm. When the elbow disappeared, Shawnee grabbed his Colt. Kennebec had reached across his body for his pistol as he spun to face Shawnee and he was raising it to fire. Lanigan drew and dived forward, rolling over. Kennebec fired at where Lanigan had been a split second before, saw the dive and the roll and thumbed back the hammer again. Before he could pull the trigger, Shawnee fired. The bullet hit his target's arm and burrowed through flesh and muscle up to the elbow. The pistol flew from Kennebec's hand and he staggered backward, crying out from the pain.

Shawnee shouted, 'That's for the dog, Kennebec.' To himself he said, *Damn! I was aiming at his chest.*

Kennebec roared with rage. He lunged toward the pistol and grabbed at it with his left hand.

'Leave it!' Shawnee shouted, springing to his feet. 'Don't pick it up!'

Kennebec bent over, raised the pistol with his left hand, clumsily thumbed back the trigger and fired. Shawnee heard a window break as he aimed carefully and squeezed. The shot hit Kennebec in the left thigh. He spun around and fell.

'That's for Ward Kincaid,' Shawnee yelled.

Kennebec rolled over and looked at his opponent. The rage had given way to surprise and dismay, but he got up to one knee and raised the pistol once more. Shawnee aimed carefully and fired a single shot. The shot hit squarely in Kennebec's heart and he fell backward and slammed into the dirt. Shawnee holstered his pistol and stepped slowly to where his opponent lay.

He looked down at the dying man and said, 'That was for Betsy Kincaid.'

Kennebec's face twisted in pain and hatred burned in his eyes. Then his face fell slack, his mouth sagged open and the hatred became a blank, sightless stare.

When blood stopped pumping from the chest wound, Shawnee took out his knife, leaned over the body, and with a few deft strokes, removed Kennebec's scalp. There were mutterings and exclamations from the onlookers.

There was a brief disturbance in the crowd when Black Hat grabbed Tomer's pistol from his hand as he drew it to avenge his friend.

Shawnee wiped the blade on the dead man's shirt, replaced it in its sheath and, holding the fresh scalp so it didn't drip on his boots, walked to where Crown waited on the boardwalk. Crown handed him the Winchester with a grim smile of respect.

'Your horse is in the stable,' Crown said.

Shawnee nodded and walked away with the scalp dripping blood into the dust of the street.

Crown glanced at the scalp hanging

221

from Lanigan's fingers. 'Damn!' he said to Black Hat. 'It looks like he just skinned a polecat!'

The big man chuckled. 'I think he did, boss.'

15

When Shawnee reached Presidio he rode directly to the marshal's office. Guitierrez looked up from his desk as Shawnee walked in and exclaimed, '*Madre de Dios*! You are alive, or is it your ghost come back to haunt us?'

Shawnee laughed and said, 'I'm still alive, a little busted up but still alive. I thought I'd stay in your town long enough to salt and cure a trophy I'm carrying and to borrow some money from you.'

Guitierrez was jubilant. 'Tell me what happened in that terrible place.'

'Buy me a shot of tequila and I'll tell you,' Shawnee said.

Shawnee stayed in Presidio long enough to catch up on his sleep, scrape and salt the inside of Kennebec's scalp and to borrow enough money from the marshal to get him back to Fort

Stockton. On his third day there, he was preparing for his trip back to Fort Stockton when Guitierrez came in smiling with a message in his hand. 'This is from your friend Milam. He is taking care of you. They have dropped the charges against you in Fort Stockton. You do not need to go back there. You are free to return home. And he says that the citizens are enjoying gossiping about the fate of the former sheriff. Would you know anything about that?'

Shawnee's trip back to Eagle Pass was a good trip. Without having to divert to Fort Stockton, he was able to follow a more direct route back to Eagle Pass. There were enough small settlements and villages along the way to spare him from a steady diet out of air-tights. The voices had retreated to some unknown dark place for how long, he didn't know. He noticed the nights were still cool but the daytime air was getting warmer. The brief Texas spring was ending and the brutal

224

summer was impatiently pushing its way in. His timing was good, he would be off the trail during the hottest part of the year.

Shawnee arrived at Eagle Pass in the early afternoon and rode directly to Brick Bryson's house. When he entered Bryson's office, he consciously tried not to swagger but his mood made it hard to conceal. Bryson stood up, glanced at the canvas bag Shawnee carried and extended his hand.

'So that prayer for the cool breeze won't be necessary,' Bryson said.

'I'm happy to say it won't.' Shawnee answered. 'Not yet anyway.'

'Well, what do you have for me?' Bryson asked, looking at the bag and raising his right eyebrow.

In answer, Shawnee opened the bag, reached in and drew out Kennebec's scalp. He laid it on Bryson's desk.

Bryson looked at it for a moment then sat down. His face had lost some of its color.

'You are a man of your word, Mr

Lanigan,' he said. He opened his desk drawer, took out a cheque book, asked how much he owed and wrote out the cheque. He closed the cheque book, called the maid and asked her to bring in Little Brick. In a few moments, the boy scurried into the room. When he saw Shawnee, his eyes lit up and he started to say something but his eyes alighted on the grisly trophy. In silence, he slowly walked to the desk. He stared at the scalp for a long while then looked up at Shawnee, then back at his grandfather. His eyes returned to the scalp; he started trembling from head to foot and suddenly broke into great heaving sobs as if his heart would break. He ran to his grandfather and buried his face in the old man's chest, shoulders heaving, crying uncontrollably.

A great wave of relief swept over Brick Bryson's face as he hugged the weeping boy to his chest. He looked up at Shawnee and whispered, 'Thank you, Mr Lanigan.'

Shawnee stood up, put on his hat, tipped it in goodbye and walked quietly out of the room.

Outside, he climbed into the saddle and said to Candy, 'There's some nice oats and a clean stall waiting for you back home. And, after I pay Sheriff Horn back the county's ten dollars, I'm going to look in on a couple of ladies out at the madam's place who have been pining away while we've been gone. Maybe, just maybe, we'll have a nice rest before we start out again on our next job. How does that sound?'

Candy tossed her head and snorted. Shawnee took it for agreement.

THE END

We do hope that you have enjoyed reading this large print book.

Did you know that all of our titles are available for purchase?

We publish a wide range of high quality large print books including:
Romances, Mysteries, Classics
General Fiction
Non Fiction and Westerns

Special interest titles available in large print are:
The Little Oxford Dictionary
Music Book, Song Book
Hymn Book, Service Book

Also available from us courtesy of Oxford University Press:
Young Readers' Dictionary
(large print edition)
Young Readers' Thesaurus
(large print edition)

For further information or a free brochure, please contact us at:
Ulverscroft Large Print Books Ltd.,
The Green, Bradgate Road, Anstey,
Leicester, LE7 7FU, England.
Tel: (00 44) **0116 236 4325**
Fax: (00 44) **0116 234 0205**

THE GUN HAND

Robert Anderson

Johnny Royal had lived on his wits and his gun after leaving home following a foolish argument. Returning home, however, he finds the neighbourhood is threatened by rustlers and outlaws. He meets a local rancher, the beautiful Sarah, whose uncle's past criminal deeds have returned to haunt them. Now, Johnny, Sarah and the ranch foreman must blaze a path of destruction against the forces searching for her uncle's ill-gotten gains, in the teeth of the outlaw's meanest gunslingers.

TOO MANY SUNDOWNS

Jake Douglas

Chance Benbow thought he had found the place — and the woman — which would bring him peace and quiet and a future. But then it all blew up in his face. When he recovered from the bullet wounds, he saw his future clearly, albeit clouded by gunsmoke. He would stride through it with a gun in each hand — and if hell waited on the other side, then he would meet it head-on, taking a lot of dead men with him.

GUN FOR REVENGE

Steve Hayes

While Gabriel Moonlight hides out
in Mexico, Ellen Kincaide asks him
to avenge the death of her sister and
Gabriel's former girlfriend, Cally.
He refuses, but when Ellen is kid-
napped by bandits Gabriel sets out
to rescue her. Then he has a change
of heart and promises to kill the man
who murdered Cally. But he discov-
ers the identity of the murderer
and knows that to exact retribution
means almost certain death. Even
so, a promise is a promise.

THE CHICANERY OF PACO IBANEZ

Jack Sheriff

When Marshal Thornton Wilde takes delivery of two prisoners, one of them is the son he hasn't seen for twenty years! Then, there is a jailbreak with Thornton and the town drunk in hot pursuit. Gradually a complicated plot unfolds involving a series of bank robberies and a Mexican peasant with lofty ambitions. Somebody is desperate to keep Wilde and the Texas Rangers away from El Paso, but it's there the amazing truth is revealed and justice meted out.

THE SHADOW RIDERS

Owen G. Irons

The Arizona Rangers give Tyrone Cannfield a tall order: he must get himself interned in an army punishment camp with hard labour and escape from the chain gang to track down the murderous Shadow Riders gang. Furthermore, alone he must bring in the gang's leader Mingo, and halt a train robbery. Yet Cannfield will do everything possible to eliminate him and the Shadow Riders — Mingo was the man who murdered his wife back in Texas . . . but can he survive?

JASON KILKENNY'S GUN

Kit Prate

Josh Kincaid was too young to be skipping school and daydreaming about dime novel gunfighters. When he found injured bounty hunter Rance Savage and brought him into town, Josh fell under the spell of a real life hero. But Savage, obsessed by an old grudge against the man who'd left him to die, was overwhelmed with bitterness. He wanted retribution. Before he realised what was happening, Josh became the mankiller's unwitting accomplice in a deadly scheme of vengeance . . .